FEUD RIDERS

Revenge for what happened to his mother burns in Jim Blackwell's mind as he seeks the father he has not seen for twenty years. Chance takes him to Mineral Wells and into a ranchers' feud, and also to the father he seeks to destroy. But as the feud riders leave a trail of destruction, Blackwell discovers an unexpected relationship with his long lost father.

KIRK FORD

FEUD RIDERS

Complete and Unabridged

LINFORD
Leicester

First published in Great Britain in 1974 by
Robert Hale Limited
London

First Linford Edition
published September 1991

British Library CIP Data

Ford, Kirk *1923 –*
   Feud riders. — Large print ed. —
   Linford western library
   I. Title
   823.914

   ISBN 0–7089–7090–7

Published by
F. A. Thorpe (Publishing) Ltd.
Anstey, Leicestershire
Set by Words & Graphics Ltd.
Anstey, Leicestershire
Printed and bound in Great Britain by
T. J. Press (Padstow) Ltd., Padstow, Cornwall

1

THERE was a frown on Jim Blackwell's angled, rugged face as he rode south from Elkhorn. His grey eyes smouldered with anger and his brain pounded, crying for revenge, as he thought of the grave into which he had just watched his mother's coffin lowered.

He tried to pluck a face from the past, but all he could remember of his father was a big man, which was a natural impression for a boy no more than four. That was the last time he had seen his father; twenty years ago.

Seth Blackwell had ridden out of Elkhorn saying there must be better places to make a living and that he would send for his wife, Mary, and his son as soon as he had found the right place. The days turned into weeks, the weeks into months and the months drifted into years but no word ever came from Seth Blackwell. Mary waited and hoped, but that hope dwindled with the passage of time. The little money she had was soon gone and she found it hard to provide for herself and her son. The only work she could find was at the shabby hotel, trying to keep it clean. The proprietor was a hard task-master, he wanted his pound of flesh, and when Mary turned down his suggestion that a little more friendliness would ease her burden he made things all the harder for her. As this was her only possible source of income she had to stick it out and bear the humiliation of the proprietor's cruel pleasure in working her hard.

There was little comfort for mother and son, but, when he became old enough to understand and help, Jim tried to ease things by doing odd jobs.

At sixteen Jim had found employment at the Bar T ranch. The foreman saw that Jim had a way with horses and he used the youngster's gift, paying accordingly. Soon Jim was earning enough to insist that his mother gave up work. But it was too late, the damage had been done. Mary's health had been undermined by the hard work and the frequent shortage of good food. The last two years had been ones of ill-health with a gradual deterioration until she had died two days ago.

Jim had gradually learnt the story of his father and how he had left Elkhorn with a promise on his lips. He had seen the bitterness creep into his mother and, though she had sometimes voiced the possibility that his father was dead, he knew she didn't believe it. He watched his mother age prematurely and hated the man who had caused it. He hated a man he could hardly remember and whom he could only recall as big. That man would have to pay!

Jim Blackwell rode slowly along the main street of Mineral Wells. The town was sleepy under the hot, Texas sun. No one walked on the street. A few cowboys lazed on the sidewalk but paid no attention to the fool who rode in the afternoon heat. Jim longed for the shade and a cool beer but first he rode to the livery stable.

A year had passed since he had left Elkhorn. A year of enquiry, searching, working and moving on. All the time he drifted south but got no nearer to finding his father. With the passing of time his need for revenge seemed to diminish and, with it, the desire to find his father, but he made enquiries automatically wherever he was. It was only when he forced himself to think of the past that it flared up again.

Once he had seen his horse cared for by the capable hands of the stableman, Jim went to the hotel, booked a room and eagerly anticipated the chance to use the bath in the shed at the back of the building.

Half an hour later in his room, a much refreshed Jim was pulling a clean shirt over his head when he heard the rumble of a wagon on the street. He

4

crossed to the half-open window and, as he tucked his shirt inside his trousers, he watched the flat wagon drawn by two horses pull to a halt outside the store. The bearded driver, whom Jim judged to be about sixty, climbed from the wagon, hitched his horses to the rail, rubbed his weatherlined face thoughtfully then entered the store.

When Jim looked out a few minutes later, as he was buckling on his gun-belt, he saw the man carrying a sack to the cart. The storeman appeared with some boxes, then they both carried two sacks from the store before they disappeared inside again.

A cowboy rode past and two men walked on the sidewalk. Mineral Wells was beginning to come to life again as some of the heat went out of the afternoon sun. Jim was about to turn away from the window when a squeak drew his attention to the saloon. Four well-built men had just pushed through the batwings and now stood on the sidewalk looking up and down the

5

street. One of them turned to the others, said something and nodded in the direction of the wagon outside the store. They all laughed and started along the sidewalk towards it. When they reached it two sat on the tailboard while the other two stayed on the sidewalk close to the open door of the store.

A few moments later the bearded man appeared carrying a box. He pulled up short when he saw the four men, then, almost immediately, he started forward again. One of the men on the sidewalk stuck out his foot and tapped the wagon driver's heels. He staggered forward, lost his balance and tumbled down the steps into the roadway. The contents of his box scattered into the dust. The four men started laughing, and the older man glared angrily at them as he tried to scramble to his feet. One of the men stepped from the sidewalk and pushed him back into the dust with his foot.

"Lie there an' watch this," he grinned.

The two men on the wagon each pulled a knife from their belts, plunged it into the sacks and slit the hessian with one swift stroke. Sugar poured out and, as it piled up, they swept it on to the road, showering it in front of the older man.

He scrambled to his feet and hurled himself at the man who had shoved him to the ground. The man side-stepped and with a sharp blow across the back sent him spinning against the tailboard. He cried out at the pain which stabbed through his body as the wood cracked his ribs. But he was given no respite. One of the men on the wagon pushed his huge hand into the man's pain-racked face and pushed him away violently, sending him sprawling in the dust where he writhed in pain.

The noise had attracted the storekeeper and his two customers, but they could do nothing as one man kept them covered with his Colt.

Jim had seen enough. Two strides took him to the door of his room. He raced for the stairs and went down two at a time. He flung open the door of the hotel and pulled up short on the edge of the sidewalk.

"Hold it!" he rapped. The unmistakable note of command in his voice caused the two men in the wagon to look up from their work of destruction. The man with the gun swung round, crouching as he did so. Jim had read the signs and in a flash his Colt cleared leather and spat viciously. The bullet took the man in his gun arm. He dropped his Colt with a cry of pain.

"Leave them!" shouted Jim, as the others made a move for their guns. When he saw that they had obeyed, Jim stepped down from the sidewalk and moved slowly towards the wagon, his eyes never leaving the four men.

The sound of the shot had really awakened Mineral Wells. People appeared on the street as if by magic and started to run towards the commotion, only hesitating and slowing to a precautionary walk when they saw the situation was still explosive. One man ignored the tenseness and the gun. He pushed his way past the onlookers on the sidewalk and ran to the figure lying in the dust. He was a man of about thirty, well built, with a face which spoke of the outdoor life. There was a ruggedness, but also a look of authority about him. Jim took him in, in one swift glance so as not to have his attention diverted from the four men. He saw the look of concern on the man's face and knew him as a friend. The man dropped to his knees beside the wagon driver.

"You all right, Matt?" he asked.

"It hurts here, Wes," replied matt holding his side. "Where I hit the wagon."

"We'll git you to the doc," said Wes. He looked up at some of the people on the sidewalk. "Give a hand," he called. Two men hurried forward. "Take Matt to the doc," he instructed and added gently, as the men stooped to pick Matt up, "Easy with him." When he

9

was satisfied that Matt would be cared for, Wes turned to size up the tense scene around the wagon.

"Is there a sheriff around here?" asked Jim.

"He's out of town," replied Wes.

"Then we'll hev to deal with these low-down coyotes ourselves, mind getting their guns?"

Wes did not question Jim. He moved forward and, careful not to get between anyone and Jim's Colt, he removed their weapons.

"Thanks," said Jim. "Wal, I guess they'd better clean up the wagon first." He glared at the four men. "Git to it," he snapped and, when there was some hesitation, he moved menacingly.

The men fell to their task and the crowd thickened as more people joined in to see what they now regarded as true justice.

When they had finished Jim spoke again. "Right, now you can load it again exactly as it was before you interfered with an old man." He glanced across at the store-keeper. "All right by you?"

"Sure, mister, sure." He hurried into the store.

Wes drew his Colt. "I'll watch 'em in the store."

Jim nodded. "Git to it," he ordered, and the four men shuffled reluctantly into the store.

Each time they appeared the crowd gave a mocking shout. When the job was finished, Jim told them to line up beside the wagon. Wes joined him and said to the four men, "I've told Zeke to charge that lot to your boss. You can do the explaining."

"Some rope," called Jim to the store-keeper who hurried into the store. Jim turned to the four men. "To your horses."

Covered by the two guns the men moved off down the street. The crowd waited and then fell in behind the procession. When they reached the animals Jim told the four men to mount but to face backwards. A murmur ran through the crowd and then someone started to laugh and soon everyone was showing their amusement. They jeered the men on the horses as Wes quickly tied the men's legs beneath their horses' bellies and their hands behind their backs. He secured them by fastening that rope to the saddle-horn.

When Wes had finished Jim slipped his Colt back into its holster. He stepped forward. "Don't let me see you pickin' on Matt again or anyone else for that matter," warned Jim.

"We'll see you in hell first," spat one of the men.

Jim grinned, untied the horses from the rail and with a whoop and a slap sent them galloping away, leaving a yelling, laughing crowd behind them.

Wes turned to Jim with a big grin on his face. He held out his hand. "Wes Clayton. My boss, Mr Blackwell, will have to hear about this."

Jim took the firm grip. His name came to his lips in reply but before he spoke the impact of Wes' words hit him. Blackwell! He was astounded. The name he thought he would never hear!

"Something wrong?" Wes had noticed the look on Jim's face. His question startled Jim, bringing him back to the immediacy of the moment.

"No . . . no. Thought there was someone in the crowd I recognized, but I was wrong. Sorry. Jim . . . Jim Benson."

Wes smiled. "Glad to know you, Jim. New here aren't you?"

"Just got in little over an hour ago," Jim replied.

"Good job you did," said Wes. "I'll stand you a drink, but I'm goin' to see what Doc has to say about Matt first, see you in the saloon."

"Mind if I come along?"

"No."

"Matt work with you?" asked Jim.

"Yeah. Running W. That's Blackwell's spread. I'm foreman. Matt came in for stores and I was in the bank when I heard the shooting. What happened?"

Jim explained what he had seen from the hotel, but his mind was trying to cope with the new information — the

Running W was Blackwell's spread. Could this be his father? Jim wanted to know more but he would have to be careful with his questions.

"Glad you saw it," said Wes. "They would have given old Matt a worse time."

The doctor reported that Matt would be all right. He had some nasty bruises and it was likely that he had cracked a rib. "He'll be all right to ride back in the wagon; gently, mind you. Let him rest here until you are ready to leave, Wes. He'll have to lay up for a few days. I'll be out to see him."

Matt thanked Jim for interfering and added, "If you're stayin' around Mineral Wells you'll have to watch out for them critters. They'll be out to git even with you."

Wes took Jim to the saloon and when they had got their drinks Wes looked seriously at Jim. "Take Matt's warnin' seriously, Jim. Those devils will try to get you," he said.

Jim smiled. "I will, but I reckon I

can take care of myself. What was it all about, Wes? I have a feeling there's more to it than just a bit of fooling around."

"There sure is, Jim. We could be buildin' up into a range war."

"What!" Jim was surprised and curious.

"When old friends fall out you can bet there'll be trouble and when it involves their youngsters it can be big. Things will happen that they'll both regret if they don't come to their senses — nobody wants a range war, with its violence and bloodshed."

Jim was hearing every word but his mind was racing with the fact that Wes had said their youngsters. This couldn't be his father.

"So this bust-up this afternoon was part of this feud?" said Jim.

"Yeah. In it's way it was nothing. Guess those four saw the opportunity for a bit of fun using the feud as an excuse."

"So they were from the other ranch."

"Yeah. The Lazy A, Pete Howley's spread."

"What did Blackwell and Howley fall out over?"

"Youngsters. Howley has a son Chuck. No good really. A big head. Likes to throw his weight about. Oh, he's tough mind you, he can take care of himself, but there's a bit of a mean streak to him. Shoots his mouth off. He attracts a bunch of young cowpokes, about his own age. When they have a night in town there'll be somebody hurt one way or another before the next morning. Wal, Chuck goes for Blackwell's daughter, Kathy, in a big way. It was natural that youngsters of friends should be around each other a lot, after all they'd been brought up more or less together but I think Chuck read more into their relationship than there was. Kathy never intended it to be as serious as he thought it was. Came as a bit of a blow when she told him there was nothing to it."

"An' I don't suppose Howley took it

16

lying down," put in Jim.

"He sure couldn't. Pressed his attentions on Kathy until she could stand it no longer and told her pa. I suppose most people in these parts thought it a natural marriage, youngsters of old friends. I know Howley hoped it would happen; he saw a joining of the two biggest spreads in these parts. Blackwell on the other hand put his youngsters first. Kathy's happiness was at stake so Blackwell warned Chuck off. Chuck persisted so Blackwell went to Howley. Didn't mince matters and thought his old friend would see to things, but Chuck is a spoiled brat who always gets what he wants, and persuaded his father to back him. Just after this Chuck was beaten up by two men. Chuck figured it was Kathy's brother, Lance, warning him to lay off Kathy, but I have my ideas."

"What are they?" asked Jim as Wes hesitated.

"Two cowpokes taking advantage of

the situation to get their own back and not get the blame, but Chuck said it was Lance, so his father had Lance beaten up and whipped. Wal that was enough to put Blackwell and Howley at each other's throats, and these things don't stay among families, they spill over on to the ranch-hands. There's a fierce loyalty to their own spreads. You've seen one little incident today, an' thet could hev been real vicious if you hadn't stepped in."

"Well, you sure look as if you'd the makings of a heap of trouble around here."

"It'll be range war unless Blackwell and Howley get some sense," said Wes. He looked thoughtful and then added, "don't know why I'm telling you all this, you'll be movin' on and it won't interest you any more. Suppose it was to explain what happened this afternoon."

"I may not be moving on," said Jim. "I was figuring on finding a job around here for a while."

"Were you?" said Wes, eyeing Jim

closely. "Where you from, what you do?"

"Dakota." Jim found himself automatically lying, as if he had some reason for keeping his origins a secret. "Been drifting from one job to another, mostly with horses."

"Horses? Got a way with them, have you?"

"I like to think so."

"Cattle?"

"Been around them; I can handle them but not the way I can handle horses."

"Wal, Jim, we could possibly fit you in at the Running W. I could hire you but I generally like the boss to have the last word. If you're interested come on out."

Jim found his pulse rate quickening. Blackwell. There was no point in getting himself stirred up. This wasn't his father. This Blackwell had two grown up children. But Jim found himself saying. "Sure, I'd like thet."

"Good. I'll go and finish my business

at the bank. See you at the doc's in fifteen minutes."

Wes finished his drink and left the saloon, while Jim mused over the situation of meeting another man with the same name as his father.

2

CHUCK HOWLEY reined his horse to a sudden halt at the top of the rise and two cowboys stopped alongside him.

They stared almost disbelievingly at the four horses moving steadily along the bottom of the valley in the direction of the Lazy A — the riders were the wrong way round!

Chuck's eyes narrowed. His square jaw stiffened. "Jed, Slim, Gil an' Blackie!" he gasped. "What the — " He kicked his horse forward. The two cowboys followed and the three men thundered down the hill.

Scared by the sound of the hooves the four horses on the trail started to move away but Chuck and his two men soon had them under control. They quickly released the four men, who tumbled from their horses and eased their stiffened hands.

"What happened?" snapped Chuck, angry that Lazy A cowboys should be in this undignified position.

Gil told their story quickly. Chuck's face showed annoyance and anger as the story progressed.

"What the hell were you doin' to let one hombre outsmart four of you? If you can't do better than that you're no good to the Lazy A. Who was he?"

"Dunno, boss," replied Slim. "Never seen him before."

"We'll know him again when we see him, and when we do he'll get what for," snarled Jed.

"Thet may be sooner than you think," said Chuck. "We'll go and find him now, teach that hombre a lesson." He looked at Gil. "You'd better go back to the ranch and git thet arm seen to." Gil nodded and climbed into the saddle. "An' when you tell pa what happened you can also tell him I'm takin' care of things."

"Sure will," said Gil, and sent his

horse off in the direction of the Lazy A.

Chuck turned his attention to the others. "A stranger helps the Running W," he mused, "it's just likely Wes will take him back to the ranch. We'll cut over to the trail they'll take an' work back towards town."

The six men put their mounts into a gallop across the grassland and soon they were topping a rise which overlooked a wide shallow valley through which ran the trail to the Running W. Chuck pulled to a halt and searched the length of the valley with a quick sweep of the eyes. A speck in the distance held his attention for a moment.

"A wagon," he said. "This could be them." He glanced back along the valley. "We'll take them there." Chuck indicated a group of hillocks which bordered the trail at a bend.

Chuck turned his horse and led the way along the hill until a spur hid them. The six men slipped over the rise and put their mounts down the slope towards the hillocks. Chuck quickly deployed his men on either side of the trail and settled down to wait.

The creak of the slow moving wagon alerted the Lazy A cowboys. Chuck signalled them and they all swung into their saddles.

The wagon came nearer. The lazy A men drew their Colts. Chuck steadied his horse and then, when he judged the wagon to be in the right position, he tapped the animal, sending it out onto the trail, with Jed close beside him.

The Running W foreman was taken completely by surprise and automatically hauled hard on the reins when he saw Chuck and Jed, with guns drawn, barring their path. Jim stiffened. His hand moved towards his Colt but stopped. He realized it would be useless with two men appearing on either side and the other moving in behind.

"Chuck Howley," muttered Wes to Jim.

Jim's curiosity and interest were raised and he studied the man who was at the root of the trouble.

24

He saw a man whose good-looking appearance could attract the opposite sex, and Jim guessed that Chuck knew it so that any rebuff from a female would go against his ego and that could spell trouble. He rode tall in the saddle. His powerful frame was well-proportioned and gave Jim the impression of a man who looked after himself. Chuck edged his horse nearer the wagon. His grey eyes flashed as he eyed Jim.

"This him, Jed?"

"Yes."

A chill gripped Jim. Matt had warned him the four Lazy A cowboys would figure on revenge for what happened at Mineral Wells but he hadn't reckoned on it happening so soon.

"Git down," rapped Chuck looking at Jim. Jim's hesitation was slight; he knew he was in a hopeless position. Slowly he stepped down from the wagon.

"See here Chuck — " started Wes, but he was cut short.

"Keep out of it, Wes. No one does

25

what he did today and gets away with it. He's all yours Jed. Brad, Mel keep them covered."

Jed grinned, slipped his Colt back into its holster, nodded to Slim and Blackie, who did likewise before climbing out of their saddles to join Jed, who had dismounted and was walking towards Jim.

Jim tensed himself. He was ready to put up a fight but if he made a play for his Colt he would put Wes and Matt in danger.

"I wouldn't try it!" rapped Chuck. It was almost as if he had read Jim's intentions.

Jim steadied himself. The three cowboys were upon him. There was a moment's hesitation as they faced him and Jim turned with his back to the side of the wagon, then with a sudden movement, Slim and Blackie leaped forward, grasped his arms and pressed him hard against the wagon.

Jed's grin revealed the delight he was anticipating as he wreaked revenge.

There was a vicious hate in his eyes when he stepped in front of Jim. He paused for a moment and suddenly swept his hand upwards. It landed across Jim's face jerking his head to the right and was immediately followed by another slashing blow sending his head to the left. Jed rained blow after blow on Jim's face. Pain seared through his face and his head thrummed madly with the sudden jerking from side to side. Cuts spread on his cheeks and his eyes began to puff.

The beating stopped. Jim opened his eyes to see Jed laughing.

"This'll teach you not to interfere," Jed hissed, and unleashed a vicious blow to Jim's stomach. He wanted to double up to try to find some relief from the pain but Slim and Blackie held him against the wagon. Three more times Jed sank his fist into Jim's middle. His brain reeled as pain seared through his body.

Jed nodded to Slim and Blackie. Jim felt his arms released and, with the slackening of the pressure pinning him to the wagon, he doubled up and pitched forward to the ground, holding his stomach, trying to ease the stabbing pain. He gasped as a boot contacted his side. He tried to roll over but another boot met him. Then, through the mists which were closing in on his mind, he heard the report of a rifle.

So intent had everyone been on the revenge beating that the rifle shot took them by surprise.

Startled by the unexpected interruption, the Lazy A men jerked round to see four riders approaching down the hillside.

"Hold it!" rapped Chuck, sensing his men were ready for a fight. "Miss Kathy's with them."

Relief swept over Wes at the sight of Kathy and three Running W men. He had felt helpless, covered by Lazy A guns, while every instinct cried out to him to help the likeable stranger, who had just got involved in Running W affairs.

The cowboy with the rifle kept it ready while the other two drew their Colts. Kathy put her horse ahead of them, and each side eyed the other cautiously, alert for any false move.

Kathy took in the scene as she approached the wagon. A bandaged Matt lying in the wagon, Wes held at gunpoint and a beaten stranger struggling to get to his feet.

With the approach of the riders, Wes ignored the guns and jumped from the wagon to help Jim. Wes got him to his feet and supported him against the side of the wagon.

Kathy pulled her horse to a halt. Her eyes blazed angrily. "Call your men off, Chuck," she snapped.

Chuck grinned. "Anythin' to oblige, Kathy." He glanced round. "All right, boys, put 'em away. We've had our revenge." He slipped his Colt back into its holster. If Kathy hadn't been there he'd have risked a shoot-up with the Running W while they were still on the hillside, but he was quite satisfied with the way things had gone. "Mount up," he ordered glancing at Slim, Blackie and Jed. He looked back at Kathy. "Know him?" he asked indicating Jim.

Kathy, annoyed at Chuck's arrogant attitude, glared back at him. "No," she replied testily. "And I don't know what this is all about but the fact that he's with Wes and Matt involves our men and I don't like to see them threatened, and then there's Matt, he's obviously been hurt, is that any of your doing?"

Chuck laughed. "You're even more beautiful when you're angry." Kathy's eyes blazed at Chuck's attitude. She fumed, trying desperately to keep control of her temper. Chuck glanced round. "Let's ride," he called, and, ignoring Kathy, sent his horse away. The Lazy A cowboys kicked their horses into a gallop, pounding after their boss, and leaving the group around the wagon with dust in their mouths.

Kathy swung quickly from the saddle and two strides took her beside Wes.

"What happened?" she asked and

before the question could be answered she glanced into the wagon. "Are you all right, Matt?" she queried, concern in her voice and on her face when she saw the bandages showing under Matt's shirt.

"Sure, Miss Kathy. I'm sorry about all this." The effort made Matt wince.

"All right, Matt, take it easy," she replied soothingly. "We'll soon get you home." Kathy turned to Wes and Jim.

Jim was breathing easier but his face was bruised and bloody. Kathy examined his face quickly. "We can't do much here," she said. "Help him into the wagon, Wes." Kathy turned and called, "Dan take my horse, I'll ride on the wagon with Wes."

Jim said nothing but he admired the way this girl had taken command of the situation. She was about twenty, slightly built but with a good figure emphasized by the Levis which fitted tightly at the waist and which she had tucked into calf-length, black riding boots. Her blouse had a low neck

31

and a bandana was tied neatly at her throat. She wore a grey, low-crowned sombrero but sufficient hair peeped from beneath it for Jim to see that it was brown with a natural curl. Her blue eyes had a tender look with them but Jim had seen them flash angrily at Chuck Howley and he guessed she had a temper when roused.

Wes helped Jim into the wagon, and he made himself as comfortable as possible beside Matt. Kathy climbed on to the wagon beside Wes who sent the horses forward.

"Well, Wes, who is he and what happened?" asked Kathy. She listened while he told his story then she turned to look at Jim.

"I'm sorry this happened, Jim, but thanks for helping Matt. I'm Kathy Blackwell; Wes tells me you're good with horses. I'm sure my father will be able to fix you up with a job."

"Thanks," said Jim. He smiled even though it hurt. He had guessed this must be Blackwell's daughter but it had made no impact on him until she had spoken her name. Kathy Blackwell, how strange to have the same name as himself. She could have been his sister.

Wes halted the wagon outside the house. It was a two-storeyed wooden building with a verandah running the full width of the front.

"Bring them inside, Wes," said Kathy as she jumped down from the wagon and went into the house.

Willing hands came forward to help Matt and Jim and, as they stepped on to the verandah Kathy appeared with an older woman.

"Mother, this is Jim Benson."

Mrs Blackwell smiled. "I'm pleased to have you, Jim. I'm sorry it's not under better circumstances."

Jim smiled. "Thank you ma'am." Jim felt the warmth from her, a warmth which made him feel at home. There was kindness and gentleness in her manner and he knew from whom Kathy got her good looks.

Mrs Blackwell directed Matt to a room and told the men to see that he got into bed. She then took Jim to another room.

"We'd better get you cleaned up first. Kathy, some hot water, please." Kathy hurried out of the room and Mrs Blackwell turned back to Jim. "Let's have your shirt off and see if any damage has been done." She saw Jim hesitate and laughed. "Now come on Jim, there's nothing to be embarrassed about. I've attended to more injured men than I care to think about and it looks as if there'll be a lot more the way things are shaping." A note of sadness had crept into her voice.

"Wes told me a bit about your troubles; I'm sorry," said Jim as he took off his shirt.

"I'm sorry you got involved," replied Mrs Blackwell. "Now let's see." She examined Jim quickly. "You'll feel mighty stiff and sore, and you're going to have some lovely bruises, but I think you'll survive," she added with a smile.

When Kathy returned with water his wounds were soon bathed and attended to.

"Where are you from, Jim?" asked Mrs Blackwell as they finished off.

"Dakota."

"Kathy told me you're looking for a job. I think my husband will have one for you, that is if you want to stay around here." Stay! Jim had found himself wanting nothing else. The nearness of Kathy had excited him. Her hands were gentle as they had bathed his cuts and her voice soft when she spoke. The Running W would suit him! "Well, Jim, I guess you'd better get into bed. Rest will do you good and the doctor can have a look at you when he comes to see Matt tomorrow. Come on Kathy, I daresay Jim can manage to eat something."

They started for the door but Jim stopped them. "Thank you both very much." There was deep sincerity in his voice.

Mrs Blackwell smiled. "It's no more

than we should do."

"I'll be up with some food in a few minutes," said Kathy and followed her mother from the room.

Ten minutes later Kathy reappeared, carrying a tray of food. She had changed into a long gingham frock. Its small pink flowers on a pale blue background accentuated her attractiveness. Her hair, now released from the restrictions of being tied up for her sombrero, fell almost to her shoulders. It shone silk-like and excited Jim when it brushed against him as Kathy adjusted his pillows when he sat up.

She sat down and, while he ate his food, talked about horses. Jim knew he had found someone who had the same stirring love for them as he had.

He had just finished his meal when the sound of hooves took Kathy to the window.

"It's pa," she said. "I'll tell him and he'll be up to see you." She picked up his tray and hurried from the room.

Jim eased himself against the pillow

and realized his heart was beating a little faster at the thought of meeting Blackwell.

Ten minutes passed before the door opened. Jim was startled. He saw a big man framed in the doorway. His impression of his father was of a big man! Jim found his mind racing, trying to tear some memory from the past which would enable him to remember his father more vividly.

"Now Jim, I've heard all about you," the voice boomed and Blackwell moved into the light from the window. Jim saw him clearly. He was big, solid, with powerful broad shoulders. His face was rugged, lined by a hard life. Here was a man who would stand no nonsense and yet Jim immediately felt from his smile of greeting that he was a man who would understand your point of view. But there was nothing to stir the past in Jim's mind, only the bigness and that was only a childish impression. "I'm mighty grateful to you for helping Matt." He held out his hand and took Jim's in a firm grip. "I'm sorry Howley's revenge came so soon."

"Couldn't do anything else, sir," replied Jim. "Couldn't see those hombres beat up an old man."

Blackwell released his grip. Suddenly Jim's brain started to whirl. He had suddenly realized what had struck him as peculiar as they shook hands. Blackwell had part of two of his right fingers missing. His mind reeled. His father had the same two fingers missing. He remembered them now; remembered a child's impression of being frightened by them. Blackwell of the Running W in Texas — the man who had left a wife and child in Montana, and had never contacted them again. He needed only one thing to verify his suspicions which whirled round in his head. He needed to know Blackwell's christian name.

"Kathy tells me you are looking for a job and you have a way with horses."

"Yes," replied Jim.

"Then there's a job for you as soon as you are on your feet."

"But don't you want to know more about me?" asked Jim.

"Kathy knows you're good with horses, you love them she says and she can tell when someone does, you both talk the same language apparently. What you did in Mineral Wells is good enough for me. I judge a man on what I know, not on his past. I like what I've seen and heard about you. That's good enough for me. Your past doesn't matter. I'll take any man on trust but woebetide him if he lets my judgement down."

The words pounded into Jim's brain. They did not sound the words of a no good man who walked out on his wife and child. Yet, those fingers.

"Thanks, Mr Blackwell." Jim found himself accepting the offer.

"Now, Seth, if you've got things fixed up I think Jim should rest." Mrs Blackwell came into the room.

"All right, Martha." He grinned at Jim. "She's always right you know. See you in the morning." He swung on his heel and strode from the room. Mrs Blackwell smiled warmly at Jim and followed her husband.

Jim stared at the closed door. The word pounded in his brain. Seth, Seth, Seth! It seemed as if his brain would burst. Seth Blackwell, a big man, with part of two fingers on his right hand missing. His father! This man must be his father!

The thing he had wanted had happened and now he felt numb. Many times he had pictured the meeting, of facing his pa, of accusing him of running out, of being instrumental in killing his ma, and then the seeking of revenge, of punishing his pa for whom he felt nothing, only contempt. But now, the moment had passed and he found he felt differently.

These people had shown him kindness. Mrs Blackwell had taken him in, shown tenderness and concern for him. She was his father's wife. To hurt Seth would be to hurt her. His father himself had shown friendliness and gratitude.

He had not appeared as a man who would leave a wife and a child stranded. Jim felt there was a deep love and respect in his family and he couldn't figure how this could come about from a man who had deliberately left a wife and son to a hard life of poverty.

Then there was Kathy. Kathy — his sister! Their true relationship hit him hard. He found himself thinking deeply about this girl and in the short time he had known her he found he was hoping she would soon visit him again. But now — his sister; that put a different aspect on things.

Then he remembered his mother and the hard time she had had. This house, this life should have been hers. She should have enjoyed the easier life which Seth Blackwell's success had brought. Instead she had been forced by poverty to work hard, to scratch and save, to suffer humiliation and finally to find an early grave. Revenge cried loud in Jim's mind, but in finding revenge he would hurt Kathy and her mother.

Jim almost wished he had never come to the Running W, had never found his father. Maybe it would be better if he moved on and forgot he had ever seen him.

The tumult which beat in his brain was suddenly interrupted by the appearance of Kathy.

She smiled warmly as she neared the bed. "Anything else you want?" she asked.

"No, thank you," replied Jim.

"Pa tells me you can have a job if you want it. He needs a good horse wrangler and someone to take care of the remuda. I do hope you'll stay."

3

"JUST carry on a normal life as far as you feel like it. Three days and you will be feeling little worse for the beating," the doctor told Jim the next morning.

Jim grinned. "Thanks, doc."

When the doctor had gone, he eased himself out of bed and dressed. It took a few moments longer than usual but the movement helped to ease his stiffness.

He picked up his gun-belt and holster from the back of a chair. He held it in his hands staring at the Colt, seeing what he had meant to do, seeing the end result of practise — the killing of his father. Jim shuddered. He found that his deep hate had been tempered. He couldn't kill Kathy's father. He would leave, ride off without a word. It would be best. He fastened his belt, picked up his Stetson and went to the door of the room. Jim glanced round and opened the door to find Kathy coming up the stairs.

"Jim! This is a pleasant surprise," smiled Kathy warmly.

"The doc said I was to move about."

"Fine."

As they reached the foot of the stairs Seth Blackwell came into the hall.

"Ah, Jim. 'Mornin'. How do you feel?" There was warmth and sincerity in Seth's voice.

"Not as stiff as I expected," replied Jim.

"Good. Decided to stay?"

Jim's hesitation was only momentary and then he found himself saying "Yes." Something told him to stay to find the answer for his father's action.

"Fine," said Seth with a smile. "Wes will fix you up with everything you want when you're ready to move out of here, but don't rush it, git yourself properly fit. Martha's and Kathy's attention for a couple of days should do you the power of good. We're breakin' in some horses, come an' look them over when you're ready."

Seth swept his Stetson from a chair and left the house. Jim stared at the closed door and wondered about the man who had just left.

"Come and have some coffee." Kathy's soft voice broke into Jim's thoughts.

"Thanks," he said.

Mrs Blackwell expressed her pleasure at seeing Jim downstairs, and poured some coffee.

"How's Matt?" asked Jim.

"Doctor says he'll be up and about in a couple of days," replied Mrs Blackwell.

"And your son?"

"Lance, he's progressing very well, thanks."

"You'll meet him later," said Kathy. "Someone told you about him?"

"Wes, on the way back from Mineral Wells. He was explaining why Matt was set upon. It's a bad business. I'm sorry."

"I don't know how much he told you,

Jim, but I feel responsible." There was distress in Kathy's voice. "I wish — "

"Now, Kathy, don't upset yourself. We've been through all this before. Nobody blames you — " her mother said.

"But, Lance, he wouldn't have suffered — "

"No, he wouldn't, but you would for the rest of your life, and none of us want that, so no more about it." Mrs Blackwell glanced at Jim. "Take her out to see the horses."

"Sure," said Jim enthusiastically. He drained his cup and left the house with Kathy.

"Like 'em, Jim?" asked Blackwell as he joined Kathy and Jim beside the corral fence.

"Sure, Mr Blackwell. They're a fine lot. I like the look of that chestnut."

Blackwell smiled. "You've got an eye for a good piece of horse-flesh. If you can handle 'em as well, you'll do fer me. We're goin' to try the chestnut first. Come on over."

By the time they reached the neighbouring corral two riders had already cut out the chestnut from the rest and were edging it towards the gate between the two corrals. The animal's eyes were lit with fire as it sought some way of avoiding the persistent riders, but every twist and turn was blocked and its only way was forward towards the fence which barred escape.

Suddenly a cowboy beside the gate flung it open and the chestnut found a way open to it. It was through quickly and galloping across the corral. The two riders followed and the gate shut behind them.

They closed with the chestnut. One of them deftly roped it round its forefeet and brought it to the ground. It struggled to get up but found the task impossible with the cowboy keeping control with his rope.

Three men jumped down from the fence and ran to the chestnut. While two of them sat on the horse's head the third slipped a hackamore on to it. A long rein of horse-hair, a mecate, was attached to the simple rawhide noseband.

The horse was allowed to get up while the two men who had been sitting on it covered its eyes with their Stetsons. The chestnut remained quiet.

Jim watched every move intently. "Just wait 'till they uncover those eyes," he commented quietly to Kathy.

A bronc saddle was fixed on the chestnut's back. The cowboy with the rein climbed into the saddle, took a firm grip on the rein with his right hand, settled himself and then nodded briefly to the two men with the Stetsons. They uncovered the horse's eyes and ran. Immediately the chestnut became a whirlwind.

It reared. Then as its forefeet came down its hind legs came up, but the cowboy held on. The horse broke into a run, its fiery eyes flashing wildly. Suddenly it stopped. The rider almost went over its neck but he held on. Then it bucked and jumped and arched its back, as it moved round the corral. Suddenly it settled giving the rider one moment of triumph when he thought he had won. The horse sensed the relaxation. It seized the moment. Its hind quarters came up sharply as its forefeet dug into the ground. The suddenness of the upheaval caught the rider unawares and he found himself flung from the saddle to fly through the air and then bite the dust.

With a triumphant snort the chestnut galloped away. The two mounted cowboys raced after it and a few moments later they had it on the ground secured by its forefeet.

The cowboy picked himself from the ground, glared angrily at the chestnut and started to slap the dust from his shirt.

"Let me try, Mr Blackwell."

"Think you should, Jim?"

"Doc said anythin' I felt like doin'."

Seth could sense Jim's enthusiasm and the desire to pit himself against this horse.

"All right."

Jim smiled and started to climb the fence.

"Kit, let him try," called Blackwell.

"Sure boss," replied Kit. "Best of luck," he nodded with a smile at Jim.

It was only a matter of minutes before Jim was in the saddle ready to signal the removal of the Stetsons.

When he was satisfied Jim nodded. The two men ran out of the way quickly.

The chestnut set off at a run, stopped suddenly and tried to propel Jim over its neck. But he was ready for it and kept his seat, balancing himself perfectly. The horse bucked and kicked. All four feet came off the ground together as it leaped, arching its back, making Jim's hold precarious, but he was not to be shaken off. The horse tried everything it knew, but with no affect on the rider. Slowly it stopped and went into a gentle walk, waiting for that moment of relaxation, which it would seize with viciousness to relieve itself of the load on its back. But Jim was aware of what it wanted. He kept a firm grip on the long rein and gave it no chance to sense a relaxation.

The moments passed as horse and rider tested each other's feelings. Then suddenly the chestnut knew the man on his back was not going to be fooled by pretence. Angrily and viciously it went into all the manoeuvres it knew to defeat the rider. Finally it leaped into the air, twisted round viciously and came down facing the opposite way. But the rider was still there; the chestnut knew it was beaten.

Jim sensed the feeling but still he did not relax. He knew the horse would try some more but now he would win. A few moments later the horse was trotting steadily round the corral giving an occasional kick.

Cheering broke out and comments on Jim's riding flowed freely. Jim smiled as he patted the horse's neck and spoke softly to it. His touch was gentle and soothing and his voice was friendly.

He kept the horse moving slowly letting it get used to a human being on its back and allowing it to feel his gentle touch on the reins.

There would still be a few more days work to do before it became a saddle horse but it would not be difficult after this initial ride.

When he was satisfied Jim slipped from the saddle and allowed the two riders to take over.

Shouts of admiration and cries of congratulation came at Jim as he reached the corral fence and climbed over it.

"Well done, Jim." There was no mistaking the pleasure in Seth Blackwell's voice. "Thet was fine ridin'. With you handlin' horses like thet we'll be able to expand this side of the ranch and go fer some army contract. After thet ridin' Wes can put you on top wages right away."

"Thanks, Mr Blackwell." Jim felt a pleasure at the recognition of his ability and sensed something which he could not put his finger on, but he knew it had something to do with knowing that the praise came from his father.

Seth turned away and started issuing orders to his men.

"Well done, Jim." He turned to the quiet voice beside him and thrilled at the deep admiration he saw in Kathy's eyes.

"Thanks," he smiled. "He's a fine animal."

"I know of a better," Kathy said quietly.

"Where?" Jim's curiosity was roused. "Same place these came from?"

"No."

"Show me."

"Right, this afternoon. Maybe pa would like you around while they tackle the rest of the horses."

"Sure," said Jim.

The work of breaking in the horses went on but, in spite of Jim's willingness to lend a hand, Seth would not allow him to do any more riding.

As Kathy and Jim were approaching

the ranch-house later that morning one of the upstairs windows opened.

"Hi, Kathy, guess thet's Jim with you."

They looked up and Jim saw a young man with a broad smile across his face. There was an atmosphere of zest which spoke of a love of life.

"Sure is, Lance," called back Kathy.

"Bring him up, I want to meet some one who can ride like thet."

Kathy laughed. "Be right with you." She turned to Jim. "Come on, meet my brother."

Jim followed Kathy upstairs wondering what she would think and do if she knew she was going to introduce brother to brother.

Jim liked Lance and he wished that he wasn't here seeking revenge.

Jim moved to the bunk-house and in the afternoon, he left the Running W with Kathy.

They kept to a steady pace towards the hills and, after twisting their way through several small valleys and cuttings, they topped a hill overlooking a long valley of lush grass lined on either side by rounded hills. Kathy turned along the hill-top and, ten minutes later, after crossing a spur, which protruded into the valley, she pulled to a halt.

"There you are," she said and pointed a short distance ahead into the valley.

Jim whistled with surprise. A huge herd of horses grazed peacefully, his eyes lit up with excitement.

"Isn't it a wonderful sight?" said Kathy. "It's a pity to deprive them of their freedom, but pa wants horses, so I expect he'll have to know about them."

"Doesn't he know about this herd?" asked Jim with surprise.

"No. I chanced on them one day. Those horses you saw today came from another herd. I've never told him about this one, because I've loved to come up here and watch them. Aren't they beautiful."

"They sure are."

"Now pa's hired you and sees a chance of supplying the army in a big way — well there you are Jim."

Jim looked at Kathy. His thoughts raced. She had shown him this herd so he could be a success, so he could impress her father with the horses he brought in.

Jim was lost for words. "Thanks," he muttered. He looked back into the valley. "The leader of this lot sure knew how to find peace and plenty to eat. Let's have a closer look at him." Jim's eyes had already taken in the lie of the land as he had been talking. "It's not so steep about a couple of hundred yards along there," he indicated. "We'll leave the horses at the top."

They turned the animals and rode slowly along the hill. Reaching the appointed place, they slid from their saddles, secured their horses, and started slowly and carefully down the slope. Half way down Jim found a vantage point behind some boulders and they stopped to survey the herd. Jim estimated there must be about a hundred with probably more beyond the two hillocks a little further along the valley.

"Wonderful," he whispered half to himself. "Wonderful sight." His eyes moved across the grazing horses. "There's some money there for your father." He glanced at Kathy and the light he saw in her eyes betrayed the love she had for the animals.

"I can't see him, Jim." Her eyes were searching the herd. A few moments later their attention was drawn to a movement on one of the hillocks. A horse broke the outline and moved on to the top. "It's him, Jim, it's him!" There was a quaver of excitement in Kathy's voice as she grabbed Jim's arm.

"Whew!" Jim let out a long low gasp of surprise. "What a beauty!" He stared in wonderment at the black which stood on the hillock.

"Isn't he magnificent, Jim?" There was admiration in Kathy's voice.

"Sure is."

They lay watching the horse. He stood proudly on the hillock, only the slow movement of his head breaking his stance. He was the king watching over his herd; the lord and master of his domain. Then his head came round in their direction. He appeared to be staring straight at them as if he sensed an intruder. He waited a few moments, then slowly made his way down the hillock, pausing once to listen. In a matter of moments he had moved along the valley away from the vantage point held by Kathy and Jim. Gradually, one by one, the herd followed.

"He sensed we were here," said Kathy.

"Yeah, and he knew we meant no harm, there was no hurry to get away, he was just being cautious," said Jim.

It was only then that they realized they were holding hands. Jim withdrew his quickly.

"I'm sorry," he muttered. He started

to scramble to his feet but Kathy grabbed his arm.

"There's nothing to be sorry about, Jim," said Kathy quietly. Her eyes were warm and soft as she gazed at him.

Jim met her look, for a moment his mind was running wild. Words poured to his tongue but he held them back. One part of him urged him to take the girl in his arms, but the other hurled the word sister at him.

Then Jim broke the moment which had seemed an eternity. "We'd better be getting back." At the same time he pushed himself to his feet. He helped Kathy but as she tried to detain him he said, "Thanks for showing me the herd," and turned away quickly to start up the hillside.

Jim's mind was pounding. The next few minutes until they were on their horses were going to be intimate. He had to help her up the slope and on to her horse. If only Kathy had not been his sister. Not a word was spoken as they scrambled upwards but, when they reached the horses, Kathy looked at Jim.

"Jim, I feel — "

"Please, Kathy, don't say anything you might regret," cut in Jim.

"Seems we both felt the same way down there. I won't regret what I'm going to say."

"You might, Kathy. You know nothing about me."

"I know the way you love horses and anyone who thinks as you — "

"Please Kathy, let's go," cut in Jim. He turned away and swung into his saddle. Kathy stared up at him. She felt annoyance but couldn't be annoyed. Before she could speak again Jim said quietly, "I'm sorry, Kathy. Some day I'll tell you why." He turned his horse.

Kathy hesitated for a moment, then climbed into the saddle and followed. There were all sorts of questions she wanted to ask but she remained silent.

As they neared the ranch Jim slowed his horse and looked at Kathy. "I hope what happened today won't spoil the friendship you have shown to me."

Kathy looked hard at Jim for a moment. Then she smiled. "Of course not, Jim. But you have a secret and I'm curious to know what it is."

4

JIM settled into life at the Running W and, in spite of the atmosphere which existed because of tension with the Lazy A, it was a happy outfit. Jim recognized the loyalty to the boss and his family and knew this could only come about because that boss was a fair, just man. And this tore at the knowledge of what Seth Blackwell had done. Could both sides of the man exist? At times Jim had to hold the locket which had been his mother's to remind him that his father had walked out and forgotten his wife and son.

When all the horses in the corral had been broken in, Jim announced to Seth Blackwell that he would bring in some more.

"You'll want some help," advised Seth. "See Wes an' take which men you want."

"I'll scout the land first and decide the best way to take them," said Jim. "I'll be away two or three days."

When Jim rode from the Running W he was troubled by his thoughts. He could leave now and let that be an end to it, but he could not forget the vow he had made when his mother died. But now he had found the man he could not kill him. Then there was Kathy. If he stayed could he prevent their feelings towards each other strengthening? With his knowledge of their true relationship he could prevent any deep affection growing on his part, but he couldn't control Kathy's feelings, and when the truth came out she would be hurt.

By the time he reached the hills he had come to a decision. Kathy liked that wild, black horse. He would catch him for her, then leave.

During the next three days Jim scouted the valley and studied the herd of mustangs. They wandered the valley in peace and Jim admired the way in which the black stallion led and kept watch, alert for any sort of intrusion.

Jim's patient observations were fruitful and, with a plan formulated, Jim returned to the Running W.

Jim was non-commital to the queries from Seth Blackwell and the ranch hands about his search for mustangs. He answered only Kathy's questions about the herd and said nothing about his plans.

The next four days saw Jim active with his preparations. He transported fence poles on the buckboard from the ranch, declined the help offered by Seth Blackwell and kept watch on the herd, particularly observing its habits when it came to drink at a waterhole. One thing pleased him — the black stallion was always the last to leave. Satisfied about the regularity of the visits, Jim erected a corral around the waterhole, leaving sufficient opening on one side to take a gate.

A nervousness went through the herd when it first saw the pole fence and smelt the unfamiliar scent of man. The black was cautious in his approach but gradually, over the next few days, as Jim's scent disappeared, and no danger was forthcoming, the mustangs became less and less apprehensive about the erection around their drinking place. During this time Jim made a gate and put it into position leaving it open. He attached a long rope to it and trailed it across the ground to a position he had selected among some undergrowth nearby.

It was on the second visit to the waterhole after Jim had completed his plans that he got his chance. Twenty of the horses, among them the black, approached the hole with confidence. They drank their fill, stayed around a few minutes and straggled out of the corral in ones and twos. Jim watched them intently, poised, with the rope in his hand, ready for action.

The black made for the gateway. There were still another three horses in the corral. Jim cursed. He wanted the black alone. Then the black turned away and trotted back to the water. Jim stared at the other three willing them to leave. If only they would come out now, Jim would have his chance. One of them snorted. The black looked up sharply, then satisfied that there was nothing wrong, went back to his drinking. Jim turned his attention to the others. Two of them moved towards the gateway, the other one stayed rubbing itself against the fence.

'Come on, come on.' Jim urged in his mind.

The first two were almost at the gate. The black looked up, turned from the water and started across the corral. Jim cursed. The third horse was still rubbing itself. The other two were at the gate and then out. The black was halfway across the corral then suddenly stopped. In that moment the other horse, seeming to sense it was being left behind, stopped rubbing and galloped after the first two horses. The black moved into the mood and started to run. Jim's nerves were tense and finely tuned to the situation. Would he have time to close the gate after the other horse was through?

"Come on, Come on," Jim whispered urgently to himself.

The horse was at the gate! It was through! Jim pulled firmly at his rope. The gate started to swing. The black was almost upon it. The gate swung faster as Jim pulled harder. It rattled shut! The stallion whinneyed loudly as it turned sharply away from the obstruction, its hooves tearing at the earth.

With a yell of triumph, Jim crashed from the undergrowth and raced to the corral. The horse galloped round the enclosure seeking the way out that had once been there. There was a broad grin on Jim's face as he secured the gate firmly.

"That's got you, my beauty," he said, admiring the horse as it shied away from the intruder. It snorted with anger and there was fire in its eyes. Jim leaned against the fence admiring it and thinking of the surprise he would give Kathy.

He left the black for the rest of the day to get used to its captivity but the following morning Jim started on his task of taming the horse. It needed all his skill and knowledge of horses but at the end of the week he had achieved his objective by using kindness, coaxing, cajoling and sympathy. In return he found he had a tough, loyal animal and he knew what delight Kathy would gain when he presented her with the horse, but he did not want to do that at the ranch. There would be too many people about. He wanted Kathy to have it before anyone else saw it. So Jim rode back to the ranch intending to collect his few belongings, take Kathy to the horse and leave for good.

Jim was still a quarter of a mile from the Running W when a rider crested the rise to Jim's right. The rider hesitated then put his horse into a gallop towards Jim. Jim halted his horse and waited. His father was sure in a hurry.

Seth hauled his horse to a halt beside Jim, "I was lookin' fer you," he boomed. "Where hev you been? Expected you lookin' fer help before now. I want to clinch a deal with the army an' I can't do thet until I get some more horses!"

There was a look of annoyance on Seth's face. Jim stiffened in the saddle.

"Well, hev you got any?" demanded Seth.

"No!" Jim answered coldly.

"What!" Seth was visibly surprised, then his face darkened angrily. "You've been gone over a week. I expected results. Don't tell me you couldn't find any. I know those hills, there are horses there. I liked what I saw when you rode that chestnut; I took you on, an' put you on top wages. I expected something in return. My men hev a loyalty; I work them hard but they know they'll get a fair deal from me. Now you can have it thet way or git out!"

Jim's eyes narrowed. He fumed under the lashing tongue and, as each word bit deep, he felt his hatred flare. This was the man who had deserted his mother; this was the man on whom he wanted revenge. The opportunity was here.

His hand strayed almost imperceptibly towards the butt of his Colt, but the movement did not escape the sharp eyes of Seth Blackwell.

"I wouldn't try it, Jim," snapped Seth. "If you aren't man enough to take a bawling out from the boss then you aren't any good to me." Seth paused, his eyes bored deep into Jim. "If you want another chance then git back out there an' bring in some horseflesh."

Seth did not wait for Jim's reply. He wheeled his horse and rode off, putting the animal into a gallop after a few paces. Jim stared after him. His father's broad back made a good target. His hand rested on the butt of his Colt, he hesitated, then pulled his horse round and stabbed it forward towards the hill country.

Jim's mind was a turmoil. What had held him back when the opportunity for revenge had presented itself? Did Seth know he wouldn't shoot? He might have thought differently if he had known who Jim really was, he might have risen to the challenge if Jim had confronted him with the truth, and then the killing would have been legitimate. But who would have believed he killed Seth Blackwell in self-defence? Seth Blackwell was respected in these parts but he was a stranger. No one would have believed him. Had that held him back, or was it Kathy?

Jim was still seething from the telling off he had received when he reached the valley. As he topped the rise above his corral he turned sharply away again. Three men were inside the corral.

Jim slipped quietly from the saddle and crept quickly to the edge of the hill. He peered over cautiously. "Chuck Howley," he hissed to himself. He quickly identified the other two as Jed and Slim. He watched for a moment. They were admiring the black which stood quietly, observing them with suspicion. Chuck said something to Jed who hurried to his horse, removed his lariat from the saddle and quickly rejoined the other two. Jim stiffened. They were going to take Kathy's horse. He slid away from the edge of the hill and hurried to his horse. After removing the rifle from its scabbard, he returned to the brink of the hill and, seizing the best moment, slid over the edge and started to work his way down the hillside, keeping his eye on the three men in the corral.

With their attention on the horse his approach went unnoticed. He chose a boulder for cover and, as the men started to approach the horse, Jim raised his rifle and took careful aim. He awaited his moment then gently squeezed the trigger. The crash echoed across the valley and dust spurted close to Chuck Howley's feet. Startled, the three men spun round, their hands clawing at their Colts but they froze as they touched them.

As soon as he loosed off his shot.

Jim jumped from behind the boulder, his rifle held ready. "Leave 'em," he yelled. When he saw he was obeyed he added, "That's sensible. Now, easy like with your left hand unbuckle your gun belts."

Slowly and reluctantly the three men did as they were told. "Now, kick 'em away," ordered Jim. When he had seen them do this Jim walked forward, but he was puzzled; chuck Howley was grinning.

When Jim reached him Chuck said, "About time you showed up; I'd just figured we'd better take the black and fix you another time."

"Well you ain't takin' the black and you ain't fixin' me. I've got the upper hand."

"'Fraid not, Jim," laughed Chuck. "You've been taped from the moment you started down that hillside and there are two rifles trained on you now." Jim stared at Chuck disbelievingly. "I'm not kiddin'. Want me to prove it?" laughed Chuck. "All right Gil, Blackie."

There was a movement behind some rocks on either side of the corral. Gil and Blackie, their rifles ready stared down the sights at Jim.

"Guess you'd better drop it," smiled Chuck. Jim glanced quickly at the two men with rifles. He realized he was in a hopeless position. He may kill Chuck but he would die too. He dropped his rifle. "Now the gunbelt." Slowly Jim did as he was told. "All right boys," called Chuck, "come on in. You too, Mel," he yelled louder and waved his arm. Jim saw a cowboy appear from the hilltop leading his own horse. Chuck laughed at the astonishment on Jim's face. "Mel watched you ride up, gave us the signal and from then on you were a marked man."

"Seems you were expectin' me," said Jim.

"Sure were," grinned Chuck, "spotted you three days ago. We were goin' to take you then but I figured you may as well finish trainin' the black fer me."

Jim stiffened. "Leave that horse alone,

Howley. He's mine. I'll hev you strung up as a horse thief."

"Don't think you have any say in the matter. Nobody will believe you even if those rifle barrels remain cold." Chuck paused momentarily. "What'll it be — killed in self-defence, resistance after horse-stealing?"

Jim was tense. He was in a spot and he could see no way out. After a year he had found his father and now he was going to die without fulfilling his revenge. If only he'd used his gun earlier. Jim's mind raced. He must play for time and hope something would give him a chance to extract himself from his precarious position.

"So you'll bring killing into your feud with Blackwell?"

"So what?" snapped Chuck.

"That'll mean more killin's."

"You reckon Blackwell thinks all that much about you. You're new, maybe he won't go as far fer a new hand as he would for one of his other men. If he does then we'll be ready for him."

Jim shrugged his shoulders. "You know Blackwell better than I do. Maybe you're right, but killin' won't really hit Blackwell very much. I know a better way." Jim had seen his chance and seized it. Now he must talk convincingly. If he could persuade Howley he also saw a chance of getting the revenge he wanted without killing his father.

Chuck eyed Jim suspiciously. "What are you gettin' at?"

"You can hit Blackwell where it hurts most if I work with you, pass you information about cattle movements and so on. You could really get at Blackwell then."

"Why should you do this? How do I know it wouldn't be a double double-cross?"

Jim smiled. "I ain't doin' it fer you, Howley; it's fer myself. I owe Blackwell fer somethin' way back."

"What?" asked Chuck.

"That's my affair," replied Jim. "I've been lookin' fer him fer a year. I found him, got a job at the Running W to await my opportunity. Now it looks as if it's come."

Chuck looked thoughtful. There could be something in what this cowboy said. Hit Blackwell so it hurt financially and Kathy might be only too pleased to marry him to save the Running W.

"All right," said Chuck suddenly. His eyes narrowed. "But let me have one inkling that you're trying to work a fast one on me — " he didn't finish his threat but there was no mistaking his meaning.

"You've no worry, Howley, I want Blackwell crippled as much as you do. There's only one thing — the stallion's mine."

Chuck Howley glanced at the stallion standing nervously beside the waterhole. "He's a beauty." He glanced at his side-kicks and then looked at Jim. "You still haven't any say in thet — "

"I think I hev," smiled Jim. "No stallion, no deal. Which is more important to you?"

Chuck glanced wryly at Jim then grinned. "All right," he said, "the stallion's yours. Now, any information fer me."

"No details. It's likely that Blackwell will get an army contract fer horses. We may be able to work on something there, but I'll let you know. Let one of your men be in the saloon in Mineral Wells each night. I'll contact him there."

Chuck nodded. "Jet, Slim you can work it between you."

Jim glanced at the two men. "It'll be three days before there's likely to be anythin' maybe longer so bide your time. An' don't contact me. I'll contact you."

Jed and slim nodded. The men retrieved their guns and, as Chuck was strapping his round his waist, he gave one final warning to Jim. "No double-cross or else — "

Jim watched the Lazy A outfit ride away, his mind toying with the situation he had created. He had no liking for

Chuck Howley nor his side-kicks, he'd find no pleasure in doing them a good turn but he had found a way to get at his father. Now he could watch him move slowly towards ruin and all that could bring, but at least he would bring no sadness to Kathy and her mother through a killing.

The whinney of a horse broke into his thoughts and he turned to see the black walking slowly towards him. Jim called softly to it, driving out the suspicion which Howley and his men had created in the animal. As he patted the animal's neck he recalled the purpose for being here. "Wal, I guess I'd better find some horses an' put myself back in Blackwell's good books."

By the late afternoon Jim had settled his ropes over two horses from the herd and when he approached the ranch-house in the early evening he saw Seth Blackwell rise from a chair on the verandah. Seth hurried to meet him and was in time to open the corral gate.

As they passed him Seth ran an

expert eye over them. He closed the gate and looked up at Jim.

"Two good lookin' animals," he commented.

"There's plenty more," replied Jim tersely.

"Good. Glad you chose to stay," said Seth.

"I'd like a couple of men with me tomorrow," said Jim.

"Sure. Tell you what, take Lance. He's itchin' to be back in the saddle. Reckon it won't do any harm now. Get Wes to fix you up with someone else."

"Right," said Jim. "I'll be in for them tomorrow afternoon."

"Goin' back into the hills tonight?"

"Yeah. Couple of things I want to do, then this time tomorrow we'll run twenty or thirty mustangs in here."

"Good," said Seth with a grin. "That's the way I like it."

Jim said no more but he turned his horse, and Seth stood watching him as he rode towards the bunkhouse. He had detected an edginess in Jim. Maybe he was still smarting from the tongue lashing he'd been given that morning. Then Seth remembered that hand straying towards the Colt. A strange action during a bawling-out. Maybe he was carrying something from the past, but Seth would not pry, he had always said a man's past did not concern him, it was what he was now that mattered. Seth shrugged his shoulders and walked thoughtfully to the house. He had a liking for Jim and figured any man who thought as much about horses as Jim did was all right. Maybe some day he would find out what lurked at the back of Jim's mind and be able to help him.

After a meal Jim sought out Wes and arranged for Dick Woods to help him the following day. As he was making his way to the stable he saw Kathy come out of the house and start towards the stable. She saw him and waved.

"Hello, Jim, wondered what had got you," she said with a smile as she joined him.

"Hello, Kathy," said Jim. "I was just going to leave a message with Matt for you. I'm goin' back to the valley now. I'd like you to ride out there early in the morning."

Kathy was surprised by the request. She looked at him curiously. "What for?" she asked.

"There's something I want you to see. But come early as I've got to be back here in the morning for Lance and Dick; they're goin' to help me bring in some more horses."

"All right," agreed Kathy, judging it best not to enquire further.

"I'll meet you on the ridge," suggested Jim.

"Fine," said Kathy. "I'll be there straight after breakfast."

"Good. I'll be waitin'."

The sun had warmed the morning air when Jim saw Kathy riding along the ridge above the valley. He put his horse into a trot and was soon turning the animal alongside hers.

"Well, where is it?" asked Kathy.

"What?" smiled Jim.

"Whatever you got me out here to see."

"Show you in a minute."

They rode along the edge of the hill, Jim guiding the way so that they came on to the valley above the corral.

Jim pulled his horse to a halt and turned to watch Kathy's face. Surprise and disbelief swept across her when she saw the stallion. She was at a loss for words when she looked at Jim. "What — What — ?"

"He's yours, ready to ride."

"What!"

"Come on." Before Kathy could say any more, Jim put his horse down the slope and Kathy was close behind when they reached the fence. They stayed in their saddles for a moment watching the black move gracefully towards them.

"He's a beaut," gasped Kathy.

They slid from their saddles and when they entered the corral the stallion hesitated, suspicious of a stranger. Jim called gently to him, and in a few moments he had accepted Kathy as she stroked and admired him with a soft caressing voice.

"Well, there you are Kathy, he's yours."

"I can't take him, Jim. You caught and broke him. He's yours by right."

"Then I have a right to give him away; besides you discovered him."

"But, Jim, I — "

"No but's about it, Kathy, he's yours. Thet's the only reason I caught him."

"Oh, Jim. Thanks is so inadequate." Before Jim realized what was happening she was against him and had kissed him on the cheek. "I'm ever so grateful."

"Want to ride him back?"

"Yes." Kathy drew the word out expressing her eager anticipation of the thrill of riding such a magnificent animal.

While Jim unsaddled Kathy's horse, she stayed with the black letting it get used to her. He saddled the stallion and helped Kathy to mount. The horse was a little nervous, but, after a few turns around the corral, it was used to its new rider. Kathy thrilled to the feel of the supple animal beneath her. There was gentleness but power in its movement and before long rider and horse were as one.

"Guess we'd better get back to the ranch," suggested Jim after a while, "or your pa will be bawling me out again."

"So this is what you were doin' when you should have been roping horses for pa."

Jim grinned. "It was worth the bawling to see you on that black."

"Not the black, Jim, he wants a name." She looked thoughtful for a moment. "Midnight, how about Midnight?" Jim nodded. "Thanks, Jim," went on Kathy. "I'll never be able to repay you."

Jim turned and walked quickly to his horse, thrusting from his mind the regret he was beginning to feel about his agreement with Chuck Howley. He hoped that this stallion would compensate Kathy for some of the anxieties she was bound to feel when he started to seek revenge on her father.

Their arrival at the ranch brought everyone out to admire the horse.

"So thet's what you've been doin'," said Seth after admiring the horse.

Jim grinned sheepishly. "I wanted to repay Kathy fer savin' me from a worse beating than I got."

"Any more like him?" asked Seth.

"There are some good ones in his herd but not one to match him. You'll see what I mean when I bring them in."

After a mid-day meal Jim, accompanied by Lance and Dick, left for the hill country and throughout the next week brought in sixty horses. Seth was pleased with the animals and told Jim to start breaking them in.

"Lance, you can continue to work with Jim, but, day after tomorrow, I want you and a couple of the boys to take those ten prize steers to the rail-head. I'm going to try to fix-up an army contract for these horses an' I want Wes with me."

Jim's mind raced. Now he had information he could use!

5

THAT same evening Jim rode into Mineral Wells and hitched his horse to the rail outside the saloon. He pushed his way through the batwings and, after a brief survey of the room, strolled over to the bar. He called for a drink and, as he took the first sip, he noticed Jed and Slim sitting at a table near the wall to his right. They appeared not to have seen him and continued their conversation with two of the saloon girls. The saloon was crowded, and Jim was casually scrutinizing the tables, from his position against the bar, when a tap on the shoulder brought him swinging round to find Dick Woods beside him.

"Hi," greeted Dick, "didn't know you were riding into town, I'd have come with you."

"Sorry, Dick," replied Jim. "Decided to at the last minute." He called for two drinks.

"I'll ride back with you, can't be too careful, Slim and Jed from the Lazy A, the two cowpokes that beat you up, are over there, they may try it again."

"Thanks fer the warning," said Jim. "I just might decide to stay in town the night," he added with a grin.

Dick laughed. "Wal now, if you want a girl to fix you up, Sally's a hot number." He indicated a girl at the end of the bar, and, before Jim could say any more, he called out to Sally.

"Hi, Sal, come over here; I want you meet a friend of mine."

Sally smiled, showing a row of white, even teeth. Jim noted a sparkle in her eyes as she walked slowly towards them. Though heavily made-up Jim guessed the girl was pretty beneath it.

"Hello, cowboy," she greeted. Her voice was soft and caressing.

"This here's Jim Benson, new horse wrangler at the Running W," said Dick.

"Hello, Sally," smiled Jim.

"You're the fella that called out those four Lazy A 'pokes a couple of weeks back."

"You've a good memory, Sally," commented Jim.

"Who'd forget the way they rode out of Mineral Wells." She laughed at the memory. "But be careful," she warned. "Two of them are over there."

"Thanks," said Jim. He called for a drink for Sally.

"Wal, I'll leave you two to get better acquainted," said Dick with a grin. "I'm goin' to find me a fortune at the tables. If you change your mind about ridin' back tonight look me up." He winked at Sally and left the bar to seek a place at one of the card games across the room.

Jim chatted to Sally until he saw that Dick had become engrossed in a card game. He had to be careful. He couldn't be seen talking to the Lazy A men, and with Dick settled to a long session in the saloon, he could not approach them here.

"Staying the night, Jim?" asked Sally.

"No," replied Jim.

Sally pouted. "Ain't I good enough? Other — "

"Sure you are," smiled Jim. "I ain't that way inclined, but I like your company an' I like you."

Sally looked thoughtfully at her glass for a moment, then she looked up at Jim and met his smile with one equally as friendly. "I thought you weren't, right from the start, but that makes no difference, I'm here to please you anyway you want, so, if you just want my company then that's all right by me."

They chatted over their drinks for about ten minutes during which time Jim decided what he was going to do.

"Sally," he said, "will you do me a favour?"

"If I possibly can, Jim."

"I want you to take a message to Jed Simmons."

Sally looked startled. "You aren't

goin' to start any trouble?"

"No," replied Jim. "I just want you to saunter over, casual like, an' when you see me leave the saloon tell him I'll be waitin' fer him in the alley to the left as he goes out."

"You ain't aiming to get your own back?" There was alarm and concern in Sally's voice.

"No," replied Jim firmly. "Any rate, what does it matter to you?"

"If there's trouble you might get hurt, and I should hate that to happen."

Jim smiled. "There'll be no trouble an' I won't get hurt, believe me." He paused, waiting for her answer.

"All right," she said.

"Another thing, Sally," added Jim. "Forget that you ever did this or that I asked you to do it."

She looked questioningly at Jim for a moment then smiled. "All right, I know when to keep my mouth shut and I know when not to ask questions, but be careful, Jim."

Another five minutes passed then Jim

whispered to Sally, "All right, leave me now."

Sally finished her drink. "See you later," she said and left the bar. She strolled among the tables edging her way, slowly and unobtrusively, towards the table occupied by the two men from the Lazy A. She kept her eye on Jim and saw him leave the saloon a few minutes later. When she glanced back at Jed she knew he was aware that Jim had left.

"Hi, Jed," smiled Sally when she reached the table. "Spare him a moment, Kitty, I have a message for him."

Kitty looked questioningly at Sally and then at Jed.

"It's all right, honey, I'll be back in a moment," Jed reassured her.

He pushed himself from the table, exchanging a glance with Slim as he did so.

When they had moved a few feet from the table Sally said quietly, "Jim Benson'll be in the alley to the left as you go out."

"Thank's, Sally," said Jed. He turned to the table and grabbed his Stetson. "Wait fer me, honey, I won't be long," he said with a smile at Kitty.

Although intent on his game Dick Woods had seen Jim leave the saloon. He thought nothing of it but alarm gripped him when he saw Jed leave a few moments later. He threw in his hand, told the other players to leave him out, grabbed his money and hurried after Jed. He glanced in the direction of Slim but he appeared to be too engrossed with a saloon girl to have noticed him. Dick slammed his way through the batwings and was only just in time to see Jed turn into the alley.

There was no one else in the street. Jim must have gone into the alley, and that was asking for trouble with Lazy A men around. Dick hurried forward, careful to move quietly as he reached the corner. Drawing his gun he stepped cautiously into the alley. It was pitch-black, and he strained his eyes trying to make out some form.

94

He moved forward three steps and stopped. A sound reached him further along the alley.

He was about to call Jim's name when something seemed to explode in his brain and he pitched forward unconscious. As he fell he struck a barrel sending it clattering against the side of the building.

The noise brought footsteps hurrying back along the alley.

"Oh, it's you, Slim," said Jed as he recognized his friend. "What happened?"

"Who's this?" asked Jim indicating the silent form face downwards in the darkness.

"Dick Woods," said Slim. "Saw him leave his card game mighty quick when Jed followed you out of the saloon. I figured he might have reckoned Jed was out to get you."

"Good thinkin', Slim," said Jed. "Don't want our set-up spoiled right at the start. Now, what news, Jim? Chuck's gettin' a bit restive."

"Sorry it's taken so long but what

I've got is worth waiting for." He told the two men quickly about the prize cattle. "Chuck can take 'em on the way to the rail-head, day after tomorrow. Lance and two hands will take them."

"Leave it to him," said Jed. "He'll fix 'em."

The two Lazy A men started to walk away but Jim stopped them. "Tell Chuck nobody gets killed or he'll answer to me!"

"Thought you wanted to hit Seth Blackwell hard, wal if — "

"Sure," cut in Jim sharply. "But no killin' or else — " He left the threat unspoken, but both Jed and Slim knew from the tone of voice that there would be heap of trouble from Jim Benson if they did not heed his warning.

"We'd better go back into the saloon separately," said Slim.

The two Lazy A men slipped away leaving Jim beside the unconscious form. He hadn't figured on Dick looking out for him; he had reckoned Dick was too engrossed in his card game but obviously Dick had been worried in case the Lazy A cowboys tried to get back at him. He regretted having to leave Dick where he was but there was nothing else for it.

Figuring that Dick could only have seen Jed enter the alley, Jim stepped over the silent form and hurried to Rosie's Restaurant a block beyond the saloon. He ordered pie and coffee and when he had finished it he made his way back to the saloon.

As he pushed through the batwings, he saw a crowd gathered round a figure lying on a table, and a buzz of excitement was evident throughout the rest of the saloon.

Jim grabbed a cowboy by the arm. "What goes on?" he asked.

"Somebody passin' the alley heard a moan, found Dick Woods from the Running W," he eyed Jim. "You just signed on there didn't you?"

"Yeah." Jim nodded and pushed his way through the crowd round the table to find the doctor examining Dick, who was just showing signs of regaining consciousness.

"Is he all right, doc?" asked Jim with an anxious glance at the doctor.

"Sure," came the reply. "It was a hard blow across the back of the head. There's a nasty gash but he'll be all right."

"Good." There was relief in Jim's voice. He looked back at Dick. "How you feelin'?" he asked.

Recognition came to Dick's eyes. "Jim!" The word came as a hoarse whisper. "You all right?"

Jim smiled. "Sure, shouldn't I be?"

"I thought — " Dick struggled to sit up.

"Take it steady," cut in the doctor. "You can talk in a few minutes. Sit up and I'll fix the back of your head."

Jim helped Dick and, as the doctor began to tend to the patient, the crowd began to disperse.

Dick winced with the pain, and steadied himself as he swayed. "Herd of cattle pounding through my head."

"All right if he has a drink, doc?"

"Sure."

Jim went to the bar and ordered a whisky.

"That gave me a shock." Jim turned to see Sally beside him. "Wondered what had happened to you when they brought Dick in."

Jim smiled. "Thanks, Sally. I'm all right."

"What happened to Dick?"

"Don't know," replied Jim. "See you later."

He took the drink to Dick. When the doctor had finished attending to the wound he advised the cowboy to take it quietly for a while before he returned to the Running W.

"I'll be with him," said Jim.

When the doctor had gone Jim asked Dick, "What happened?"

"I saw you leave the saloon; just after that Jed left. I thought he might be after you so I followed. I saw him turn into the alley beside the saloon. I took about three paces into the alley, heard nothing, then wham! I got it."

"Jed?" asked Jim.

"Don't know. I don't think it could have been. I'd hev sensed him there, or seen him; I was only just in the alley. I figure it was somebody behind me." He looked thoughtful, then suddenly his face brightened. "Slim," he said. He was with Jed." Dick glanced round and called to Sally.

When the girl came over she asked, "You all right, Dick?"

"Sure," grinned Dick. "Sally, you were talkin' to Jim, he left, then Jed left, I followed. Did anyone else leave the saloon after me?"

"Yeah. Slim." The words were out before Sally caught Jim's warning glance.

"There you are, I knew it. Where's those two Lazy A coyotes?" he looked round the saloon angrily. "There!" He started to push himself to his feet.

"Steady on, Dick." Jim restrained him. "You're in no condition to pick a quarrel."

Dick slumped back on his chair. His legs felt watery. "Guess not," he muttered. "But I ain't forgettin' this. I'll get the coyotes before long."

"All right, but simmer down now," said Jim. He was anxious to know what Dick had seen and how much he had heard or surmised. "I'm sorry if it was my fault," he added, hoping he had given Dick a lead, "but thanks for being concerned about me."

"That's all right," replied Dick. "Got to look after Running W if Lazy A are about. Did you see Jed or Slim?"

"No," said Jim. "I went to Rosie's for somethin' to eat. They didn't come in there."

"Funny, I wonder why Jed was goin' into the alley? I figured he was after you."

"Not me," said Jim.

Half an hour later Dick said he felt fit to ride. The two men left the saloon and rode at a steady pace to the Running W where there was an immediate outcry against the Lazy A with promises being made to Jed and Slim.

Lance and the two Running W hands, Kit and Glen bunched the cattle closer as they entered Red Rock Gulch. They were moving steadily and were about halfway through the gulch when the quietness was suddenly shattered by the crash of a rifle. One of the steers let out a loud bellow, ran a few yards then crashed to the ground. The others started to run. A volley of rifle-shots reverberated through the gulch. Cattle screamed and hit the dust.

At the first shot Lance's horse whirled. Startled by the unexpected and by the sight of the steer falling, Lance glanced in the direction of the shot. Alarm stared from his eyes. As the other shots echoed around him he sent his horse for some cover. He swung from the saddle and yanked his rifle from its scabbard. The other two riders were close behind him.

"Up there!" yelled one of them pointing to the far side of the gulch.

The three men raised their rifles and loosed off a volley of shots, but no answering fire came. A few more bullets were sent from the rim of the gulch at the cattle.

"They ain't interested in us," cried Kit. "I can git across the gulch, maybe git one of them from there." He leaped to his feet and, before he could be stopped, he broke cover.

"Kit!" yelled Lance. "It isn't any — " He cut his words short realizing it was too late. Kit was away at a crouching run. "Cover for him!" Lance shouted and the two men started a rapid fire towards the rim of the gulch.

Suddenly Kit's rush was stopped as if he had run into a wall. Then he staggered a few paces, pitched on to his face and lay still.

Lance and Glen stared at the silent form and Lance cursed between grim lips. The firing stopped. The two men waited tensely, then, as they heard distant hoof-beats fading, they came from behind their cover and ran to Kit.

Glen turned him over hopefully but the spreading blood across his chest told its story of finality. His eyes narrowed with hate as he looked up at the top of the gulch. "The bastards!" he hissed.

Anger welled in Lance. His eyes searched, hoping to find some movement. His rifle was ready. All he wanted was some sign. But there was none. Their ambushers must have gone. "Damn the Lazy A!" he snarled. "They'll pay for this."

"You think it was — ," started Glen.

"Who else?" replied Lance tersely. "It was the cattle they were after; they weren't interested in us until Kit made a move. Nobody but the Howley's would be interested in slaughtering our cattle; they'd do it to get at us." He stood up and grimly surveyed the bodies strewn along the gulch. Ten prime steers, which would have brought good money, lay in worthless heaps. "C'm on, Glen, we'd better git back. I should hate to be in Howley's boots when pa hears about this."

They retrieved their horses, swung Kit's body over his saddle and headed for the Running W at a fast pace.

Kathy, who was on the verandah of the house, was the first to see the riders approaching.

"Dad! Lance is back, looks as if there's been an accident," she shouted through the open door.

The alarm in her voice brought Seth and his wife hurrying on to the verandah.

Cowboys ran to meet the riders. Questions flew as they crowded round when Lance and Glen pulled their sweating horses to a halt.

"What happened, Lance?" queried Seth.

"Bush-whacked in Red Rock Gulch," replied Lance. "Kit and all the cattle killed."

"What!" gasped Seth, and a murmur ran through the group crowding round the horsemen.

Ice-cold fingers gripped at Jim's

throat. He had feared the worst when he saw Kit's body but he hoped it had been an accident. His mind was numbed as Lance's words bit into him. Lance's voice seemed to be far away yet every word was clear, making an impression on Jim.

So Chuck Howley hadn't heeded his warning. There would have to be a day of explanation, but Jim was relieved that it had not been Lance.

Willing hands took the body away.

"You never saw your attackers?" pressed Seth, seething with anger at the assassins.

"No, pa. They obviously were there to kill the cattle. Must have been the Lazy A."

"I reckon," snapped Seth, his mouth set in a grim line. "Let's find out."

Words sprang to Martha's lips to stop them but she kept them to herself. She had seen hard times and knew men's whims would pay no heed to a woman. Now this whole affair could blaze into a real range war. As the men strode away to get their horses, she turned to Kathy. She saw the alarm and horror on the girl's face. "Come, Kathy, all we can do is wait."

"But, Ma, we must stop them. There will be killings and all because of me." Kathy started after the men but Martha grasped her arm and restrained her.

"It's no use, Kathy. They'll have to go. Your pa didn't like it when I persuaded him not to take revenge after what happened to Lance. Now with this on top of it, we wouldn't be able to stop him. And it's not your fault, Kathy."

"But it is, Ma, if I'd agreed to marry Chuck none of this would have happened."

They watched the twelve Running W riders headed by Seth and Lance leave the ranch at a fast pace.

Not a word was spoken until they started down the slope towards the Lazy A, and Seth began to slow the gallop. He noted the effect of fourteen riders, suddenly appearing over the skyline, on the Lazy A cowboys. They left their various jobs and moved along the corral fences on either side of the path leading to the ranch-house. They spaced themselves out, eyeing the riders with suspicion.

"Wes," called out Seth. "Hold just short of the hombres. Lance and I will ride in."

Wes acknowledged the order and, when he judged a position which put them in gun-shot range, he called to his men to halt.

Seth and Lance kept their horses to a trot and rode steadily between the two lines of Lazy A men. Although father and son appeared to take no notice of them, both were ready for one suspicious move, but all they got was silent hostility.

Word had gone into the house, and Pete Howley and his son appeared on the verandah. They eyed the two riders who now approached at a steady walking pace. Then tension built up with every step and there was a charged silence when Seth and Lance halted their mounts close to the verandah steps. Seth matched Pete's stare as anger flashed between them but Seth's was tempered with hate.

Seth swung out of his saddle and slowly mounted the four steps on to the verandah. His eyes never left Pete Howley.

"The men who killed Kit and my cattle, I want them!" Seth's voice was quiet, cold but full of determination.

"I'll give you five minutes to git out of here!" Pete's voice was threatening.

"When I git the bastards who slaughtered my steers," snapped Seth.

"I don't know what you're talkin' about," replied Pete coldly.

Seth's arm swept viciously. His hand slapped Pete's head backwards and the power of the blow sent him staggering across the verandah to stumble over a chair and fall heavily. The sudden unexpectedness of the blow took everyone by surprise, and Seth had stepped forward, towering menacingly over Howley, almost before anyone realized what had happened.

Chuck's hand flew to his Colt but Lance, alert for any move, was ahead of him. His Colt cleared leather and his voice rasped, "Leave it!" as Chuck's hand closed on the butt of his gun. He froze and glared at Lance. "Ease away from it!" ordered Lance and Chuck slowly let his hand move away from the Colt to his side.

Lance could feel the tension intensify behind him. Any moment he expected all hell to break loose, but nothing happened. Each side viewed each other suspiciously, awaiting some move by their bosses.

Seth glared angrily as Pete pushed himself to his feet. Deep hatred burned in Pete's eyes as he fingered the trickle of blood from the corner of his mouth.

"Those men!" hissed Seth.

"Which men? Which steers?"

Seth fumed. "I did nothing after you whipped Lance for something he didn't do. Martha saved you then, but Kit an' this slaughter on top of that whipping — you're goin' to git paid for both if I don't git those men."

"Hold it, Blackwell!" Chuck's voice rasped as he realized his father was in an awkward position. "I haven't told pa yet. Kit wasn't my doin', it was an accident."

Seth swung round. "You! You no good — " Seth spluttered as his eyes blazed with anger. Then suddenly he exploded. His hand swept viciously against Chuck's face. Chuck staggered backwards to crash against the wall. Seth was on the younger man before Chuck realized what was happening. He drove his fist hard and deep into Chuck's stomach and, as he began to double up, Seth brought his left hand viciously upwards into Chuck's pain ridden face.

Alarm and the desire to protect his own showed on Pete's face. His hand started for his gun, but his glance swept to Lance and saw the menacing Colt pointing in his direction. He was helpless to stop the blows which were pounding into Chuck's face, lacerating, cutting until blood spurted. Chuck pitched forward off the wall falling into unconsciousness, and, as he did so, Seth brought both fists hard across the back of his neck sending him crashing to the boards face downwards.

Breathing heavily Seth stood over him. A wild streak of viciousness blazed from his eyes, almost as if didn't know what he was doing. Pete yelled at him but Seth didn't hear him. Alarm seized Lance as he realized this was not the end, that his father was going to go on beating the man who had admitted killing the steers. Lance knew he must stop him, and knew he would have to risk a gun fight to do so. He swept his Colt skywards and pulled the trigger.

The sudden shock of the shot seemed to jerk Seth back to reality. As the gun blazed hands moved to their Colts but no gun cleared leather for the cowboys on both sides realized what was happening.

Seth stared at Chuck for a moment,

then he glanced at Pete. "He killed my ten prize steers in Red Rock Gulch," he panted. "Thet ought to send a shudder down any cattleman's spine, but I guess not yours." There was contempt in his voice. He turned and climbed into the saddle.

Pete moved to his son and dropped on his knee beside him, looked at the bloody face and then looked up at Seth through eyes smouldering with anger. "I'll git you for this, Seth!" he hissed.

Seth ignored the threat. "Tell him if he tries to pull anything else like that he won't get off so easily." Seth swung his horse and stabbed it forward putting it into a gallop past the Lazy A men, who lined the path, just waiting for the signal from their boss. Lance, with his gun still drawn to act on the first wrong move he saw, was close behind. But there was none, and Seth and Lance reached the Running W riders without incident. The men whirled their horses and put them into a gallop behind Seth and Lance.

Back at the Running W Seth raised a point during their meal, which made the rest of the family wonder.

"Was it generally known that we were goin' to move those prize cattle this morning?"

"Only amongst our own men," replied Lance.

"That's what I thought," mused Seth. "Then, unless one of them talked, how did Chuck Howley know we were moving them?"

"Maybe it was coincidence," suggested Martha. "Maybe he just happened to be passing that way."

"No, Ma," said Lance. "It was a set up. They were waitin' for us."

Alarm showed on Kathy's face. "Then you mean we have someone amongst us who is working with the Howley's!"

6

JIM was still angry at the killing as he rode at a steady pace towards the Lazy A in the gathering darkness that same evening.

Lights gleamed from the ranch-house and the bunk-house but there was no one about as Jim rode up to the Lazy A. Jim halted his horse at the ranch-house, slid from the saddle and went to the door. He stopped and rapped sharply on it and without waiting for a reply, flung it open and strode inside. He crossed to the door on his right and, as he shoved it open, he was met by an astonished Chuck.

"What the — ?" Chuck started.

Jim brushed past him into the room. Pete Howley jumped from his chair, astonished by the intrusion.

"Who the devil are you?" he snapped angrily.

Jim ignored him and swung round to face Chuck. "I warned you, Chuck," he snarled. "I've a good mind to break you in two."

Chuck's lips tightened. Annoyance smouldered in his eyes. "It was an accident," he replied.

"I said no killin'," rapped Jim. "I figured you'd hev an excuse. But don't let it happen again, or I'll git you, accident or not."

Pete came between the two men. "What's this all about?" he snapped. He glared at Jim, his eyes narrowing. "Threatening my son can get you into a heap of trouble. I'll hev you — "

"Hold it, pa," cut in Chuck.

Pete swung round on his son. "You defendin' what he's done?"

"No, but maybe he had a right."

"What!" stormed Pete. "He had no right to burst in here an' throw threats about."

"I had every right when your son broke his bargain," put in Jim sharply.

"Bargain? What bargain?" Pete glanced

from one to the other. "Who are you any way?"

"Jim Benson, if the name means anythin' to you. I take it Chuck hasn't told you."

"No, he hasn't," snapped Pete, "but the name does mean somethin'. You're the new horse wrangler at the Running W." His eyes narrowed and his voice went cold. "And let me tell you any Running W man is poison around here now, so I reckon — "

"Hold it, pa," broke in Chuck. "Jim's workin' with us."

"What?" Pete looked disbelievingly at his son.

Chuck told his story quickly.

Pete started to chuckle. "It sure is a good set up. I'd like to see Blackwell's face if he knew what was happening." He grinned broadly. "We'll hit the Running W so hard Seth will have to give way." He looked hard at Jim. "What's your interest in Blackwell? Why are you looking fer revenge?"

"Thet's my business," replied Jim, coolly.

Pete hesitated for a moment then said, "All right, I'll not pry so long as it works to our advantage."

"It will," promised Jim.

"Good, anythin' else in mind?"

"Yeah. Blackwell is goin' in fer sellin' horses to the army. We've got sixty head we'll be movin' in about a week's time."

Chuck grinned. "We'll hit thet lot, pa."

"Sure."

"Could bring us in a good few dollars," added Chuck.

The look of pleasure disappeared from Pete's face. "It won't," rapped Pete. "Where's your sense? If we suddenly trade horses we're condemning ourselves, and branding ourselves as horse-thieves. All we're interested in is bringin' Blackwell to his knees, not makin' money on the side. Got that?"

"Sure, pa, sure."

"Yeah, an' see these side-kicks of

yours know it too. Don't be tempted to keep any of those horses. In fact we'll make sure no one does. If we hit them just before they drop down into Lee Valley we can turn them west along the rim to Eagle Point an' drive them straight over the edge."

"You don't!" snapped Jim. "No one treats horses thet way!"

"You ain't got any say in how we do it," rapped Pete.

"Then you don't get to know when we're movin'."

"We can watch."

"Then no more information."

Pete glared at Jim. "So what do you propose to do?"

"Two miles before we reach the place you suggest we move through Horn Pass. There's plenty of rocks and boulders and a few of these sent down the right moment will panic the horses and block the way for the riders I'll be holding back. We can't git to the horses so your men placed at the end of the pass will be able to fall in

119

with them and turn them into the hills and scatter them. That way none of the Lazy A need be seen."

Pete nodded thoughtfully.

"Good idea, pa?" said Chuck excitement in his eyes.

"Sure. We'll do it thet way Jim, give us the date."

"Don't know it yet but I'll let you know. Usual way?" he added looking at Chuck.

"Right."

Jim turned to the door but was stopped by Pete. "Have a drink before you go, cement a partnership. I'll like to know more about yourself."

"I guess you would," said Jim without feeling. "I'd better git back. I took a risk comin' here."

"I wondered about thet," said Pete.

"Oh, I was careful," replied Jim. "But I ain't makin' a practice of it, unless you make a practice of killin', then I'll be here again and it won't end up as friendly as this meetin'!"

Jim did not wait for any answer but

hurried from the room leaving father and son wondering about the horse wrangler from the Running W.

Jim rode in the direction of Mineral Wells but swung across country so as to make his approach to the Running W along the trail from town.

The next four days were spent in breaking in the rest of the horses. Lance spent a great deal of that time helping Jim and the two men developed an understanding which deepened their friendship. Lance quickly picked up much of Jim's skill and Seth was pleased at the way the team was developing; he saw in it a new source of wealth, for the army had promised him a contract if his first delivery proved satisfactory.

"They're a good lookin' bunch," commented Seth when Jim and Lance came from the corral after breaking-in the last of the mustangs. "They should clinch the contract. We'll move 'em out tomorrow. You two take a couple of men."

"Can I ride along with them?" asked Kathy.

Jim waited anxiously as Seth hesitated over his decision. His mind raced. If Seth said yes he couldn't inform Howley when the horses were being moved. Withholding the information may bring trouble and suspicion of double-cross but he couldn't endanger Kathy.

"No, Kathy, I'm sorry," said Seth, unaware of the relief his answer brought to the man standing close-by. Kathy started to protest but her father stopped her. "After what happened to those steers it could be risky for you to go."

"You think they might try for the horses?" said Kathy with some surprise.

"You never know," replied Seth. "We can't be too careful. I'm goin' to send Wes and six men as escort. Not to help with the herd," he added looking at Jim and Lance. "They'll keep you in sight but won't be in the way."

When everything was ready Jim rode from the Running W and turned in the direction of Mineral Wells when he was out of sight of the ranch. He had ridden three miles when he heard the pound of hooves behind him. Jim cursed when he saw Kathy; now he had been seen. He halted his horse and Kathy brought Midnight alongside him.

"Hi," she greeted. "I was exercising Midnight and was about to turn for home when I saw you. Going into town?"

"Yes." replied Jim.

"I can ride a couple of miles with you and still get back before dark. Mind?"

"No."

Kathy smiled with pleasure and they sent their horses forward together.

"Wish I was coming with you tomorrow," said Kathy.

"I'm glad you're not."

"Jim!" The girl looked taken aback.

"No, I didn't mean it that way; but there could be danger."

"I suppose so." Kathy looked thoughtful. "Everything would have been all right if I'd married Chuck, maybe I should, even now."

"No, Kathy, no!" The words came out venomously almost before Jim had realized it, but the thought of Chuck married to Kathy nauseated him.

Kathy stopped her horse sharply. "Then you do care! Jim, I thought there were times when you purposely avoided me."

Jim had stopped too. He looked embarrassed, and was annoyed with himself for creating such a situation by hastily spoken words. He looked hard at Kathy. "Remember when we first went to look at the mustangs in the valley?" Kathy nodded. "Well, the situation hasn't changed since then."

"But, Jim, you care, you like me. I know. I can tell from your reaction when I mentioned marrying Chuck," protested Kathy. "What is it? Why do you hold off?"

"I can't tell you, Kathy?" replied Jim. "Some day maybe." Jim turned his horse and stabbed it into a gallop along the trail.

For one brief moment Kathy almost

put the black after him but she held back. Annoyance, anger and bewilderment at the mystery seethed in her as she watched the fast vanishing figure galloping across the prairie. Then she turned her horse and rode slowly towards the Running W. The anger welled inside her and she suddenly kicked the black into a gallop, hoping the exhilaration and the thrill of the powerful animal beneath her would rid her of some of the anger she felt towards Jim Benson.

Jim had purposely arranged an early arrival at the saloon hoping he would be there before Jed and Slim. A swift glance around the room told him he had judged correctly. As he reached the bar Sally left one of the tables and crossed the room to join him.

"Hello, Jim," she said. "You haven't been in for a while, thought you'd forgotten me."

Jim smiled. "Couldn't do that, Sally." He called for two drinks. "You've got a room here haven't you?"

"Yes." Sally was a little surprised at Jim's question after their previous meeting. "You feeling — ?"

"Not that, Sally."

Sally pouted. "I could fancy you, Jim. You said I seemed different and you were right. I just need someone like you to take me out of here and if I have to entice you — " She left the sentence unfinished and said, "Come on, let's go." She drank her whisky in one gulp and started towards the stairs.

Jim tossed his drink down and followed. Sally led the way to a door at the end of the balcony and went into the room. Jim stepped inside and closed the door behind him. He took in the room in one swift glance. It held a bed, the top covering of which was a patchwork quilt, a wardrobe, small table, an upright chair and one easy chair. Two small tattered carpets half covered the wooden floor.

Sally sat on the bed and indicated a chair to Jim. "Want a drink?" she asked.

"Thanks."

Sally poured two glasses and as she raised hers, she looked hard at Jim. "To you, although I can't make you out. I know a dozen fellas who'd be pleased to swop places with you."

Jim looked at Sally seriously. "Sorry, if I disappoint you."

Sally looked thoughtful for a moment. "Deep down I don't think you do. Maybe I admire the good, clean-living type. I was once until — " her voice faltered momentarily, then she tossed her drink back and resumed her saloon girl outlook. "If you haven't come up here for love what have you come for?"

"I'd like to use your room for a private meeting."

Sally looked curiously at Jim. "Who with?" she asked.

"Jed — "

"What!" Sally broke in with surprise. "Lazy A, Running W, what goes on between you two?"

"Sally, there's no need for you to

know; better if you don't. But I figure you can keep your mouth shut. No one must know about this."

"Sure," replied Sally. She pushed herself from the bed and kissed Jim. "I'd do anything for you — anything." She smiled with a twinkle in her eyes as she straightened. "I suppose you want me to bring him up here when he comes in."

"Yes."

"All right, if you don't want my company now, make yourself at home. I'll be back with Jed."

Jim held her hand as he she turned away. She stopped and looked at him. "Thanks, Sally," he said sincerely. "I'll not forget this."

When Sally went out Jim pushed himself from the chair and stretched himself on the bed. He relaxed and mulled over the situation. For Kathy's sake he wished he had never seen the Running W but, as he forced himself to remember a lonely grave, he knew he must seek revenge even though Kathy got hurt, but that hurt would solve the relationship Kathy was creating. Maybe he would be back for Sally.

Half an hour later the door opened and Sally came in with Jed close behind her. Jim pushed himself on to his elbows and nodded at Jed. Sally hesitated and then, catching Jim's look left the room. Jim swung from the bed.

"Well?" asked Jed. "Boss is gettin' impatient."

Jim eyed Jed. "If he wants to play things this way he'll hev to learn to be patient. I can't rush Blackwell."

"All right, all right," said Jed irritably. "Got somethin' now?"

"Sure. We drive the horses tomorrow."

"Good." Jed's eyes gleamed with the thought of the excitement which would come.

"One thing, it may not be as simple as Chuck expects. Blackwell is sending Wes Clayton and six men as an escort."

"Won't make any difference now we know," rasped Jed.

"They won't be riding with us, an'

129

I can't tell you where they will be in relation to the herd."

Jed frowned for a moment, then he grinned. "Don't matter, we'll fix something."

Jim eyed Jed firmly. "Remind Chuck, I want no killin' unless it comes to a gun fight which can't be avoided."

"An' that can always be arranged," laughed Jed.

Jim grasped him by the arm as he turned to go. His eyes were cold as they stared into Jed's. "I mean it," he said quietly. "If I find anyone steps out of line in this respect they'll have me to answer to."

Jed grinned, shook his arm free and left the room.

A few moments later Sally came back. "Jim," she said with some alarm and concern in her voice. "Be careful. I don't like that look on Jed's face and he's more than useful with a gun. You've already crossed paths and he won't forget it even if you're working together."

Jim smiled and patted her shoulders. "I'll be all right, Sally, don't worry. Now, anyone from the Running W in the saloon?"

"Not when I came up here," she replied. "I'll have another look now."

She slipped out of the room and returned a moment later. "No one," she said.

"Good."

They left the room and to create an impression, Jim put his arm round her shoulders. They laughed and talked as they crossed to the bar. After one drink Jim left the saloon and rode back to the Running W.

The following morning there was great activity at the Running W, as Jim, Lance, Charlie and Hogan, prepared to leave for the army post. At the same time Wes Clayton and six ranch hands were getting ready for their escort duty. Seth Blackwell was bustling everywhere; instructing Lance about negotiations at the army post, giving last minute instructions to Wes and showing concern about the horses to Jim.

"How far is Wes ridin' with us, Mr Blackwell?" asked Jim as he was about to swing into the saddle.

"All the way," answered Blackwell. "He isn't leavin' until ten minutes after you, so no one will know the route he's takin, not even you nor any of your party."

"Fair enough," said Jim. He glanced round. Lance and the two riders were in the saddles. "Looks like we're all ready, Mr Blackwell."

"Good. Best of luck."

Jim swung into the saddle and sent his horse over to the corral gate. A cowboy awaited his signal to open it while two others were ready to send the horses out of the corral.

"Right, let 'em come!" yelled Jim.

The gate swung wide and as the horses came out they were kept under control skilfully by Jim, Lance, Charlie and Hogan. They kept the horses bunched tightly until they were clear of the ranch when Jim allowed them to string out as the tight control relaxed. Dust swirled and rose skywards, and shouts of good wishes came from Wes Clayton's party.

Ten minutes later Seth Blackwell gave the order to Wes Clayton and his posse to move out. Wes then led them away from the Running W in an easterly direction so that he could use the higher ground from which to keep a watch on Jim's herd.

He would not have felt so confident had he known of the cowboy who had watched the whole proceedings through a spyglass from a hill a mile from the ranch. When he was satisfied as to Clayton's intended route the man slid away from the hill-top and ran to his horse. Once in the saddle he put his horse into a gallop towards Horn Pass.

When he reached a pre-arranged place on the high ground on the west side of the pass he found Chuck Howley and the Lazy A cowboys all ready there. Chuck grinned as the man gave him the information, then he issued instructions quickly.

"Jed, you stay this side with me, Slim, Gil you take the other side an' place the dynamite directly opposite ours, you know the spot." The two men nodded. Chuck turned to the Lazy A foreman. "Red, take the rest to Luke's Hollow. Clayton's party will have to pass through there. You can hold 'em up an' give us time to set the dynamite off."

The foreman acknowledged the instruction and the Lazy A men rode off quickly to their appointed tasks.

As the horses moved steadily towards Horn Pass, Lance turned his animal and rode to join Jim on the opposite side of the herd.

"Ought we to send Charlie and Hogan ahead to see the horses don't spread out too much as they come out of the pass?" Lance called.

Jim shook his head. "They'll be all right. I want Charlie and Hogan back here to pick up any horses that stray too far up the sides of the pass. Could lose some horses that way."

Lance nodded. He was surprised but said nothing. He figured if they pressured the horses, moved them more quickly, they would practically eliminate any chance of them straying.

A few minutes later Lance saw Jim speak to Charlie and then ride to have a word with Hogan. Both men fell back and took up their positions on either side of the pass and gradually moved up the slope ready to deal with any strays.

Jim kept his eye on them and was satisfied that they should be in no danger from the expected rock fall. Jim glanced across at Lance. He was riding close to the horses. The pass began to steepen. Jim figured the Lazy A attack should come soon. Hogan was way back picking up a couple of strays but Charlie had had no trouble and was closer. Jim waved indicating him to drop back and help Hogan. When he saw Charlie ride away, Jim turned his horse towards Lance and, a few moments later was edging alongside him.

"Ease off, Lance," yelled Jim. "Don't press 'em, let them make their own pace through here."

"But — ," Lance started.

"Ease off," cut in Jim roughly, showing annoyance that his order should be questioned. At the same time he slackened his pace thus forcing Lance to do likewise or disobey the man bossing the drive.

As he turned away, Jim sensed Lance's disapproval but he had no alternative. He could have sent Lance back too but it would have looked too suspicious.

Jim eased his pace even more as they moved further into the pass. He cast an anxious glance upwards to the top of the rocky, boulder strewn heights. Any moment now he expected to see boulders rolling down. He looked across at Lance, Jim cursed. Lance seemed to have edged nearer to the horses again. He saw Lance turn his head in his direction. Jim waved beckoning him over but, before Lance had time to turn his horse the whole world seemed to erupt.

Two ear-shattering explosions came from the sides of the pass high above them. Jim's horse shied but he kept his seat and the whole scene came to him in one vivid flash. The herd seemed to pause for a fraction of a second and then was away in a terrified gallop, away from the explosion and the falling rocks. Jim saw great rocks heaved from the heights of the pass and spewed outwards and downwards a short distance ahead.

Lance, startled by the suddenness of the explosion, lost control of his horse as it shied. The frightened animal turned too quickly, lost its footing and crashed to the ground pitching Lance from the saddle. The breath was driven from his body but he scrambled to his feet only to see his horse had been quicker. Before he could make a move towards it the animal was galloping away. Lance started to run. Rocks pounded into the ground a short distance behind him, shaking the earth beneath his feet.

As he turned his horse, Jim saw Lance fall and lose his mount. He checked his animal and skilfully turned it again. Almost in the same movement he stabbed it forward into a gallop towards the running figure.

Lance was out of danger from the main fall as it sent dust skywards and blocked the pass, but Jim saw the danger from the minor falls of earth and rocks crashing away from the rim of the canyon and avalanching towards them.

Jim yelled to his horse and the animal responded. It seemed to Jim that he would never close the gap, then suddenly he was leaning from the saddle sweeping Lance up behind him as the horse slowed. Lance grasped eagerly at the helping arm and almost before he was behind Jim he felt the horse surge away. Its hooves tore at the ground in its eagerness to get away from the terrifying row of tumbling boulders and flying rocks. Every second seemed eternity to the two men; every moment they expected to be engulfed. Rocks and stones flew close-by. Jim and Lance crouched, willing the animal faster. Then suddenly they were safe. The pounding still continued as rocks and earth heaped behind them, but missiles no longer whistled close to them. Jim's horse seemed to sense the relief in the two men on its back and felt their relaxation. The pace eased and in a few moments Jim was pulling the animal to a halt.

"Thanks, Jim," said Lance. "I owe you my life."

Jim acknowledged Lance's comment with a smile and a friendly slap on the shoulder as they dismounted. Hooves pounded as Charlie and Hogan galloped towards them. There was concern on their faces as they pulled to an earth tearing halt and yelled, "You all right?"

"Sure," replied Lance. "Thanks to Jim."

"Yeah, saw the whole thing," said Charlie. "Thought you were a gonner when your horse fell." He eyed the animal which Hogan led by the rein. "Doesn't seem any the worse."

"Thanks fer stoppin' him, Hogan," said Lance as he took the reins from the cowboy. He looked along the pass at the great heap of boulders and rocks that blocked it. "Thet sure puts paid to Horn Pass. Pa ain't gonna like this — we've lost all the horses; any chance of findin' them Jim?"

Jim shook his head and pulled a face. "They'll scatter in these hills, it'll be hopeless to try to trace them."

"Then I reckon we'd better git back an' break the news to pa." He glanced at the tops of the pass. "Very neatly done," he said. "But I sure wouldn't like to be in Howley's boots."

"You figure it was the Lazy A?" said Jim.

"Who else?" replied Lance, answering question with question.

"Suppose so," said Jim.

Lance looked thoughtful. "What puzzled me is the fact that they knew we were comin'. Thet was dynamite they used so they'd been ready."

"Seems the boss's idea of an escort didn't pay off," commented Hogan, as they turned their horses and set off for the Running W.

"Wes was too late to stop this happening but maybe he saw who did it," replied Lance. "Let's go." He stabbed his horse into a gallop and the four men thundered out of Horn Pass.

They were half way to the ranch when a group of riders broke the skyline of a rise to their right.

"Wes!" exclaimed Lance. The four riders pulled their horses to a halt and waited.

Relief crossed Wes Clayton's face when he saw the four men were all right.

"I'm sure glad to see you," he said as

the riders milled around. "Thought you might be under that lot in Horn Pass. Sorry we weren't there to stop it."

"What happened?" asked Lance eyeing the dishevelled appearance of the Running W men.

"We rode into Luke's Hollow to be met by a cross-fire. We were pinned down there, no chance of getting out." His face clouded angrily. "They knew, Lance, they knew."

"Anyone hurt?" asked Lance.

"No. They were content to keep us there. They left us as soon as they heard the explosion. By the time we got our horses it was no good pursuing them, and, realizing the explosion had come from the direction of Horn Pass, we were concerned about you."

"Did you see who they were?" asked Jim.

"Sure. They were Lazy A."

A murmur of agreement came from the rest of Clayton's party. Some added their opinions about seeking revenge on the Lazy A.

Wes calmed them and turned to Lance. "Well, you hear them," he said. "What is it to be?"

"There's nothin' I'd like better to git after those bastards," he said, "but this whole thing has been so well planned that I figure it might just be what they want. We might just walk into a trap. We'll git the Lazy A later. Pa had better know about this right away, his army contract's more important now. There might be a chance to save it if we git back quick an' help Jim bring in some more mustangs." Lance's words were firm, crisp and commanded respect. The Running W cowboys saw the sense in them and as Lance set his horse forward they fell in with him at a fast pace.

7

THE noise, created by the pounding hooves of the Running W riders, brought Seth Blackwell hurrying on to the verandah. His eyes widened with astonishment when he saw the men whom he expected to be well on the way to the army post.

"What is it, Seth?" asked Martha as she and Kathy, attracted by the noise, hurried out of the house.

"It's Lance, Wes, Jim, everybody back," replied her husband, a note of apprehension in his voice.

"Trouble!" gasped Kathy. Her eyes scanned the group of riders quickly. "There's something to be thankful for, everyone's there."

"Thank goodness," whispered Martha.

Seth's knuckles showed white as he grasped the rail of the verandah tightly, trying to keep a grip on himself until he heard the news, for already the Lazy A and Howley were hammering in his mind.

The horsemen stirred the dust as they pulled to a milling halt in front of the verandah.

"Well, what happened," boomed Seth impatiently.

"They hit us in Horn Pass," replied Lance, and went on to tell his father about the ambush.

When he had finished his story Seth looked sharply at Wes. "Where were you?" he boomed harshly. "You were sent to protect that herd."

Wes told his story quickly and Seth listened without comment.

Throughout it all Jim watched Seth carefully, secretly enjoying every squirm, every annoyance, and the pain he felt at losing his horses. At least this was some revenge for the suffering his mother had felt.

By the time Wes had finished Seth was fuming. "All right, one of you git my horse. We'll hit the Lazy A so hard they won't trouble us again." He started for the verandah steps.

"Hold it, pa!" Lance's call stopped Seth dead in his tracks. Annoyed at the delay he spun round. He frowned and faced Lance grimly. "We could hev done that, pa," went on Lance, "but I figured the Howleys might want us to do just that; we might be ridin' into a trap. They'll be ready for us in any case, after our visit when they killed the steers. If we get crackin' and help Jim we can get some more mustangs quickly. I reckon if you ride over to the army post and explain the reason for the delay an' tell the authorities thet we'll hev the horses there in record time they might just play along, give you another chance to fulfil the contract before they look elsewhere for the horses."

As Lance had been speaking some of the anger had subsided in Seth and he began to think more clearly. He pondered a moment when his son had finished then he looked at Jim. "Reckon it can be done?" he asked.

"Sure," replied Jim convincingly.

"Right. You can all get some grub, then be ready for whatever Wes and Jim want. And, Jim, thanks for savin' Lance. I'll not forget it." The riders started to move away. "Wes, I'd like to see you a minute." Wes halted his horse and slipped from the saddle. Seth waited until the other riders were out of earshot. "Sounds to me like the whole affair was planned."

"Sure was," agreed Wes.

"Then it'll pay us to look into this carefully. You eat with us." He turned to his wife. "Can we manage another one?"

"Certainly," said Martha. "It'll be ready within ten minutes."

"Right," nodded Wes, and led his horse away for the stableman's attentions.

When they were all seated at the table Seth came straight to the point. "It's obvious this thing was planned, but the big question is how did Howleys know when we were movin' the horses and where to?"

Wes glanced up sharply. "Yeah! And that there was goin' to be an escort!"

Everyone grasped the meaning of Seth's words but it was Kathy who voiced them. "You mean somebody tipped them off? Same as we thought after the cattle were slaughtered."

"Yeah, but we realized people outside the ranch would hev known when we were movin' those steers; this is different. The decision to move the horses with an escort was made only later yesterday. The only way the Howleys could know was by a tip-off from someone on this ranch."

"But all our men are loyal," said Martha.

"We would guess so but it seems we must be wrong."

"Couldn't someone have been keeping a watch on the ranch?" suggested Kathy.

"Sure, but that wouldn't tell him where we were headin'," said Lance. "They were waitin' fer us. They must hev known in order to get that dynamite set up."

"How did they know we'd go through Luke's Hollow?" said Wes.

"Now, thet's why I figure someone was watching the ranch, not to find out where the herd was heading, they knew that already as Lance has pointed out," said Seth. "I reckon the real reason was because someone had told them there was goin' to be an escort an' they wanted to know which route it would take," explained Seth.

"Once they knew thet," said Wes, "they'd realize we would pass through Luke's Hollow and so they settled to hold us up there while the dynamite was blown."

"Right," agreed Seth.

"Then it's obvious that someone tipped them off, otherwise they wouldn't hev known about the escort," said Lance.

"And they wouldn't hev known to watch the ranch longer than the departure of the herd."

There was silence round the table as

the real significance of the situation bit into their minds.

Seth glanced round the table. "We've got to check on everybody to see who left the ranch after I'd decided to send the horses today." He looked at Wes. "Can you check the men?"

"Sure. Might be best to do it right away before we leave, then we might be able to stop any more disasters," said Wes.

"Right, but we'll start round this table." Seth saw the looks of surprise on everybody's face. "Now, don't start objectin'. I know everyone here is in the clear but to get a proper picture and to be fair to all the hands it's only right we should account for ourselves. Now I know Martha and I didn't leave the ranch. I can't account for anyone else."

"You're right, father," said Kathy. "I for one left the ranch after your plans were made." All eyes turned on Kathy. "I exercised Midnight."

"See anyone, talk to anyone?" asked her father.

"Yes. I was about to turn for home when I saw Jim Benson heading for town. I rode with him for a short while before I returned here."

Seth nodded. "So we know Jim Benson went into town. There's no need to ask him, Wes."

"We don't know that he actually went into town," pointed out Lance.

"True," said Seth. "What about you, Lance?"

"Didn't leave the ranch, pa. Spent some time with Matt in the stable then came into the house. Didn't go out again."

Seth nodded and glanced at Wes.

"Wasn't off the ranch, boss," said Wes. "Got involved in a poker game with Charlie, Hogan an' Glen."

"So thet clears all of them," said Seth.

"Sure, Glen said he intended goin' into town but he stayed in the game too long an' changed his mind."

"Right, can you check the others?"

Wes nodded and as soon as he had

finished his meal he left the house. He returned ten minutes later.

"No one left the ranch," he announced. Kathy gasped when she realized where this put the suspicion. Seth frowned.

Lance knew what everyone was thinking. "But, pa, Jim saved my life."

Seth nodded. "I know, that's what I keep remindin' myself. But does thet prove he didn't tip off the Howleys?"

"Guess not when it comes down to it, but would he have bothered about me?"

"Who knows? He was the only one who left the ranch. It's likely he went to town."

"But not definite," cried Kathy. Her brain whirled with the implications against the man she had come to think so much about. She clutched at some possible escape for Jim.

"Agreed," said her father. "He could have turned off the trail and gone to the Lazy A."

"Or he could have met someone in

Mineral Wells," put in Wes.

"Surely it couldn't be Jim," Martha said. "He seems such a nice young man. Besides he was beaten-up by Lazy A men. He wouldn't side with them now."

"Yeah, I know," agreed Seth. "Whichever way you look at it there's always something which points the other way. But remember we know nothing about his past."

"Then let's get him in here and find out," suggested Lance.

Seth hesitated a moment, then said, "Wouldn't do any good. He would lie. No, we need proof, besides, talking of lying, any one of the men could have lied about not leaving the ranch yesterday."

"Then, what are we goin' to do?" asked Lance.

"Only one thing to do. Act as if we weren't suspicious, carry on normally, an' keep an eye on Jim Benson."

There was silence for a moment. No one liked to point the finger of suspicion of spy on a man they had come to respect and admire especially for saving Lance's life and for the way he handled horses.

Seth glanced round them all. "Anythin' else to add?"

"Yeah," said Lance, "though I hate to do so. Two things. Jim didn't handle things in Horn Pass as I would have done. I made a suggestion about sendin' Charlie and Hogan ahead but Jim rejected it." He went on to explain the happenings at Horn Pass.

"Wal, I would have done what you suggested," said Seth. "If you are implyin' he deliberately held back then it also implies that he would have known what was goin' to happen and wanted that rock to fall between the horses and you."

"So no one would git hurt," said Lance, thoughtfully. "You know I had pushed up nearer the horses again. Jim had just waved to me to fall back when the explosion occurred."

"Mm," Seth looked thoughtful for a

moment then said sharply. "What was the other thing?"

"Wal, Jim was in town just before the steers were killed. Remember it was the night Dick got bushwhacked in the alley next to the saloon. Dick said he thought Jed Simmons from the Lazy A was going after Jim so he followed. Then he reckons it was Slim who got him."

"But Jim had been to get somethin' to eat," protested Kathy, alarmed at the way evidence seemed to be piling up against Jim.

"It's hard to put any time on these happenings," said Seth. "Jim could have been with Jed; Dick didn't see anybody in that alley. Jim could hev gone for somethin' to eat after Dick had been bushwhacked. No one could prove that he wasn't eating when Dick was hit. We can't prove either one, but I reckon we'd better keep an eye on Jim."

"I'll do that," said Wes.

"Good. Now we'd better see if we can salvage anythin' out of the mess.

Organize as many men as Jim wants; I'll ride over to the army post and explain the situation."

"Take someone with you," said Martha.

"I'll be all right," laughed Seth.

"The way things are, you never know," Martha pointed out.

"All right," replied Seth wanting to ease his wife's mind. "I'll take Dick Woods. It'll give me another chance to have a chat about thet night in Mineral Wells."

Twenty minutes later, Seth Blackwell and Dick Woods saw the rest of the outfit head for the hills, then mounted their horses and left for the army post.

Wes and Jim organized the Running W cowboys to get as many horses as quickly as possible. Estimating it would save time if Jim, with help of Lance and himself, could start breaking horses immediately they were brought in, Wes had some of the men erect another corral, next to that used by Jim for Midnight. Luck was with the Running W, the herd was not far away from the corral and by sundown they had taken twenty horses.

Their speedy progress towards recovery would have dampened the hilarity of Chuck Howley and his sidekicks who were celebrating their success at Horn Pass, in the saloon in Mineral Wells.

"Another couple of hard-hittin' raids an' I figure Seth Blackwell will be really feelin' it," said Chuck to Jed with a broad grin. "An' maybe Kathy will be glad to marry me to save her father."

"But thet don't mean you'll git the Running W," said Jed. "There's Lance."

"If he should happen an accident, I would," said Chuck.

Jed grinned. "Some fella might be worth rewardin' if Lance happened to — "

"He just might," cut in Chuck.

"What about Jim Benson's threat?"

"He's servin' a purpose; after that, well accidents can happen to the best of people," replied Chuck. "Know anythin' about him, Jed?"

"No," answered Jed. "But there's somethin' about him thet don't ring right."

"I know what you mean," said Chuck. "Wonder why he wants to harm Seth Blackwell?" He looked thoughtful. "A complete stranger rides into Mineral Wells, gits a job at the Running W and immediately is prepared to sell Blackwell out. It can't be because of anythin' that happened since his arrival. Must be somethin' from the past. I'd sure like to know."

"I don't think he'd appreciate me asking him," grinned Jed.

Chuck laughed. "Reckon not. You told me Sally acted as somethin' of a go-between between him an' you."

"Yeah."

"Well, maybe she's the person to use her charm on Benson and find out."

Jed nodded. "I'll fix her."

Chuck smiled. "It'll be worth her while."

Half an hour later Jed saw his opportunity and when he had got Sally a drink at the bar he casually dropped his question.

"This fella Benson, know anythin' about him?" he asked.

"No."

"Know where he comes from? Or anythin' about his past?"

"No."

"He's said nothin' that might help?"

"Not a thing."

"All he asked you to do is to contact me on the two occasions?"

"Yes."

"You ain't talkative, are you?" said Jed.

"I'm answering your questions and that's all there is to say. I can't tell you any more because I don't know any more."

"Think you can find out?"

"Dunno," replied Sally. "Look here Jed, what's all this about? What you want to know for?"

Jed hesitated a moment. "I'll level

with you, Sally. I know you can keep your mouth shut. Benson wants to get at Blackwell so he's sellin' him out to us. Now Chuck would like to know why."

"Oh, so that's why you an' Jim haven't clashed as I reckoned you would after the way he made you ride out of town."

"Don't remind me," winced Jed. "I won't forget — my turn will come. Chuck is playin' for high stakes, he'll pay you well if you can find anythin' out. But keep this to yourself, Sally."

"As you say, I know when to keep my mouth shut."

The following afternoon, Seth was pleased with the situation when he and Dick Woods joined the Running W men. Seth brought cheering news that, provided he could deliver thirty horses within the week, the army would honour the contract and take delivery of the rest a week later.

"Figure you can do it, Jim?" asked Seth.

160

"Sure." Jim looked thoughtful for a moment. "Five days if we stay out here to break the horses."

"Five days," said Seth. "Wednesday today, then we move on Monday. Good. You, Lance, Wes, Dick, can all break horses, Charlie and Glen to help. If you've got all the horses you want, the rest of us can return to the ranch."

Wes and Dick nodded. "Next batch thet the boys bring in should do it," said Wes.

"Good, I'll wait to see them," said Seth. While the work went on, Seth, pretending to examine the horses sought the opportunity to inform Lance and Wes what he had learned from Dick Woods.

"I got him to think back to go over every detail of that night, missing nothing, no matter how trivial."

"Did you learn anythin', pa?" asked Lance, hoping for something which would clear Jim.

"Wal, nothing conclusive, but somethin' we might be able to work on if watching Jim doesn't give no proof, one way or the other," replied Seth. "Dick introduced Jim to Sally, left them talking at the bar when he went to join a card game. He saw Jim go out. Next thing, he saw Jed leavin' the saloon. Dick left the game immediately, he remembers glancin' back. Slim was still at the table with a saloon girl, but Dick seems to remember seein' Sally nearby." Seth paused to see if these words meant anything to Lance and Wes. When he got no reaction he went on. "If Dick's impression is right it might give us a lead. I looked at it this way; Sally was talkin' to Jim, she was in the vicinity of Jed's table when he left, is it possible that Jim sent a message to Jed through the girl?"

Both men saw his point. "Jim wouldn't want Dick to see him talking to Jed, so he gets Sally to tell Jed to meet him outside," said Lance thoughtfully.

"Could be," replied Seth, and Wes nodded his agreement. "It's no proof, I know, but maybe Sally would talk. It could be worth lookin' into."

As Wes had predicted the next batch of horses which were brought in gave them sufficient from which to get the first thirty required by the army. Satisfied that they were making sufficient progress to beat Howley's attempt to prevent him fulfilling the army contract, Seth rode back to the Running W with the men not required to handle horses.

During the next two days Jim sought some excuse to leave the working party. He needed to get word about the new arrangement to Chuck Howley. Preventing this new batch of horses from reaching the army would hit Seth Blackwell hard. It would lose him the army contract, an important source of revenue which he was banking on.

On the three occasions he tried to slip away he felt he was being watched and after the third time, he suspected Wes Clayton was his shadower. An uneasy feeling, that suspicion had been cast his way, gripped him. Yet outwardly everything seemed to be all right. There was no easing in the friendliness of Lance or Wes or any of the other Running W hands. There was nothing Jim could really put his finger on. He must exercise caution but he must get his information to Chuck Howley.

It was late on the Saturday when the opportunity presented itself. Wes had just dismounted from one of the horses in the corral when the animal reared and caught Wes on the forehead with one of its hooves. The foreman crashed to the ground unconscious. Lance, who had been watching from the fence leaped down and raced to Wes, yelling to the others as he did so. He was on his knees beside the unconscious man when they reached him.

One glance was sufficient for Jim. "I'll get the doc," he yelled and raced out of the corral to his horse.

The sound of hoofbeats pounding away into the gathering darkness suddenly struck Lance forcibly. Jim was heading for town and the man who should be following him lay unconscious! Lance leaped to his feet.

"Take care of Wes," he called, and ran from the corral.

Jim kept to a fast gallop. He must get help to Wes as quickly as possible, but he saw this as an opportunity to contact Jed or Slim in the saloon and strike the biggest blow yet at his father. Jim's mind was filled with the possibilities and he was so pre-occupied that he almost missed the sound of a galloping horse as he slowed to cross a stream.

Jim did not slacken his pace until he reached the edge of town. There he eased it to listen, but only for a moment. The hoofbeats were nearer! The unknown rider had gained on him! Jim rode quickly to the doctor's a block beyond the saloon on the opposite side of the street. He was out of the saddle almost before the horse had stopped and ran quickly to the saloon.

Pushing through the batwings, he was glad to see Sally just leaving one of the tables. As he crossed to the bar, she saw him and read an urgency into his look.

"Sally, go outside an' see if anyone from the Running W rides up," panted Jim. "If so, let me know straight away; I'll be out at the back."

Sally nodded and went quickly to the batwings. Jed and Slim at their usual table, had noticed the hurried conversation between Jim and Sally and were surprised to see her go out at the front, while Jim made his way quickly to the back door. As he passed their table Jim indicated to Jed that he wanted him to follow.

Jim had barely stepped outside before the door opened again and Jed was beside him.

"Something wrong?" he asked.

"I think I was followed," said Jim. "Soon know when Sally gets back."

"Someone on to you?" asked Jed.

"Don't know, could be. I've had a feelin' I'm being watched, so we'd better wrap this up quick. Now listen carefully. The army hev given Blackwell another chance. He's movin' thirty horses on Monday. I reckon he'll guard 'em well this time so here's what I propose to hit Blackwell hard. You fire the prairie to stampede his cattle and head 'em for Eagle Point. That'll take all the hands from the ranch an' I'll see we all leave the horses. Then you can scatter them."

Jed grinned. "Good idea. That'll sure bring Blackwell to his knees."

"Right," said Jim. "Fire on Sunday morning. You come back here and I'll let you know the result."

The door opened and Sally stepped outside. "Lance Blackwell," she said.

"Git back in the saloon, Jed, quick." There was an urgency in Jim's voice. "Go in with Sally as if you'd just been outside with her."

Jim didn't wait for a reply but raced away along the alley. After covering two blocks he cut down to the main street. Keeping to the shadows he stepped on to the sidewalk and paused. A swift glance along the street told nothing except that his was still the only horse outside the doctor's. Lance had not come that far. He altered his position so he could see the saloon. Jim stiffened. The light from the windows lit up the figure of Lance Blackwell, as he looked into the saloon. So Lance had followed him. The Running W were suspicious.

With Lance's attention on the saloon, Jim seized his chance. He ran swiftly across the street, moved quickly in the shadows to the doctor's, and was soon tapping at the door which was out of sight of the saloon. His knock was answered and he quickly told the doctor his reason for being there.

When Lance reached Mineral Wells he slowed his gallop so as not to attract attention. His eyes searched the gloom for any sign of Jim but he saw none. Dismounting a block from the saloon, he walked along the sidewalk, noting that there was a horse outside the doctor's, but at this distance he could not recognize it. Reaching the saloon he peered cautiously through the first window, but saw no sign of Jim. The window beyond the batwings would give him a better view of the whole room so Lance shifted his position. He surveyed the room thoroughly. Lance felt some relief when he did not see Jim. Had they been mistaken about him? Lance hoped so; yet evidence seemed to point Jim's way. He had to check him out. Lance saw Jed and Sally sitting down at a table. A few moments later Jed got up and started towards the batwings.

Lance realized he must not be seen. If there was anything between Jed and Jim, Jed might pass on the information that he had seen Lance in town, and that would make Jim suspicious. Lance moved swiftly away from the saloon and took up a position in the shadows opposite the doctor's. He saw Jed come on to the sidewalk, hesitate and then lean against the rail. Suddenly there was activity across the street. The doctor appeared leading his horse from the stable at the rear of his house. Jim was with him and, when both men had mounted, they rode out of Mineral Wells. Lance knew his ride had proved nothing conclusive. It was just conceivable that Jim could have passed a message, but he would have had to be quick, and, as far as Lance could prove, Jim had been at the doctor's all the time. Now Lance would have to get back to the camp before Jim and the doctor. He moved into the nearby alley and quickly made his get away round the back of the saloon to come back on to the main street near his horse. He glanced in the direction of the saloon. No one leaned on the rail. Lance climbed into the saddle, rode out of town and put the horse into a fast gallop, cutting across the prairie to beat the two riders ahead.

As Jed went back into the saloon with Sally the fact that Lance Blackwell was in town preoccupied him. Could he take his chance to get rid of him for Chuck?

170

He pondered the matter as he sat down and came to the conclusion that this was not the time. Killing Lance now would only raise a wide investigation and might spoil the plans suggested by Jim. Jed decided he must wait until after tomorrow, Seth Blackwell would be hard hit, things would be going Chuck's way, and then it would be the time to get Lance out of the way. Unless there was the chance of staging an accident now. Jed told Sally he would be back shortly and left the saloon to take in the situation outside. He saw no sign of Lance Blackwell and a few minutes later, after he had seen Jim ride out of town with the doctor, he returned to the saloon.

Lance was relieved when he rode into camp to find that Jim and the doctor were not there. He was also relieved to find that Wes had regained consciousness and appeared to be all right. Warning the other three men to say nothing about his absence from camp, he quickly unsaddled his horse and was sitting with Wes when Jim and the doctor arrived.

The doctor examined Wes thoroughly and announced that he would have nothing worse than a huge lump and a severe headache, for a day or two, but advised him to take things quietly for a week.

"I'll see he goes back to the ranch first thing in the morning," said Lance.

"Best place for him," the doctor agreed.

The following morning, in spite of Wes's protests, Lance insisted that he return to the Running W.

"You'll mend quicker with care and attention from Ma an' Kathy. Besides you can tell pa about my trip into town and warn him that it might hev been possible for Jim to tip off Jed about movin' these horses, but as far as I can prove he only went to the doctor's."

Lance sent Charlie with the foreman and the rest of them to set to work on the corralled horses. Jim showed his dissatisfaction with several of the horses, which surprised Lance for Jim had already looked them over and approved them.

"We can maybe git four better ones," Jim suggested.

"But we haven't time, we've got to take these animals to the army tomorrow," pointed out Lance.

"We could do it if the herd's not too far away. It'll mean a better price for your pa," replied Jim. "I'll take a look from the top of the hill."

Lance said nothing, but as he watched Jim ride up the hill he wondered what the horse wrangler was up to. Lance held himself ready to ride should Jim disappear from view.

When he reached the top of the slope, Jim stopped to survey the valley. He had seen what he wanted to see when he topped the rise but he waited a few moments before yelling to the men below.

"Lance! Dick! Glen! Get up here quick!" The obvious urgency in Jim's voice sent the men running to their horses, and his frantic waving made them put their animals up the slope as quickly as possible.

When they reached the top and halted their panting horses alongside Jim, they saw the reason for his panic. Smoke curled up in a great cloud across the distant prairie!

Lance's eyes widened with horror. "We've got a big herd of cattle over there!" he gasped.

"What!" Jim feigned surprise.

"If they're the wrong side of the fire they'll be trapped on Eagle Point!" said Dick.

"And that means only one thing — the herd is finished!" yelled Lance. "Let's ride!"

He put his horse into an earth pounding gallop, and, as he followed suit, Jim smiled to himself. Soon he would see his father really suffer and his revenge would be complete.

8

THE four men kept the horses to an earth tearing gallop. Lance hoped that the herd was safe but when they topped a rise his heart sank. There were no cattle on this side of the fire. They must be trapped between the inferno and the escarpment.

"Got to git to the other side," he yelled.

"We'll hev to try to git round one end of the fire," shouted Jim, hoping to delay things a little longer.

"There's a gap there," shouted Lance, indicating a small gap in the flames. He stabbed his animal forward and found it answered to his urgency. Earth flew as they tore towards the gap, with Lance hoping the flames would not close it before they were through.

A tremor of fear ran through his horse but Lance kept it pounding onwards.

Now he could feel the heat intensifying. The flames crackled louder. The gap was closing. Smoke choked him. He was close to the flames, which seemed to rise higher and hasten their rush to devour him. Then he was through, with the earth pounding behind him as Jim, Dick and Glen held their horses in a dead run close to him.

The four men hauled hard on their reins taking in the situation as they swerved to avoid frightened cattle. They saw bewildered steers, trapped between a fiery death and the steepness of an escarpment which spelt doom. They turned and ran and turned again, seeking some means of survival. The smoke hung thick, blotting out much of the scene beyond, as the gentle wind took it across the landscape.

The four men saw riders bunching together a short distance away, and, as they sent their horses towards the group, Lance saw his father amongst them. The disheveled riders, their faces streaked black from the smoke, endeavoured to keep their frightened horses under control as they milled around Seth, who was shouting his view of the situation to them. He had no time to acknowledge the newcomers except with a nod.

"We can get out and leave the cattle here," he yelled. "Save ourselves and see them die by fire or in the plunge over the escarpment. Or we can make one last, desperate bid to save them. If we lose them the Running W is finished. I won't hold it against anyone who leaves now." He paused but not one man turned his horse away. "Thanks," he shouted, but no one doubted his true feelings when they saw his face and the look in his eyes. Smoke blew around them smarting their eyes bringing tears, which marked paths down their cheeks through the blackness. Seth went on quickly. "This escarpment turns at right angles at Eagle Point. There is still a gap between the fire and that part of the escarpment. Our only hope is to use it. Drive the cattle towards Eagle Point and turn them there to go through that gap. It'll be tricky. We'll hev to move the herd fast and they've got to be turned at Eagle Point. I want five volunteers to place themselves at Eagle Point. They'll hev to face a herd of frightened cattle and turn them — use your guns, kill if you have to but turn the cattle — if not you won't stand a chance you'll go over the edge with the steers." He stopped, waiting for an answer.

"I'll go, pa," yelled Lance.

"Count me in." The call came from Dick Woods.

Seth's eyes met Jim's. Jim held back. Why should he risk his neck for the man he sought to destroy? Why should he try to save his cattle? Seth looked away as three more men called out.

"Off with you," yelled Seth.

As they galloped away Jim saw the glance which Seth gave Lance, and he wished it had been for him. In it there was love, respect and admiration for a man who had not flinched from a danger which might mean death. That look could have been for him.

Seth was making his final orders. Two men were sent to the gap not closed by the fire. They were to use their slickers to try to hold back a spread of flames which would close that gap and trap the herd. "Right, now let's move those cattle."

Quickly the riders turned their horses and spread out with Seth taking a position nearest the escarpment. Jim found himself next to his father. Steer bunched against steer, bellowing in anger and in fright. Cowboys yelled and slapped their Stetsons. After what seemed an age, but in fact was only a few minutes, the cattle started to move quicker. The cowboys exerted more pressure. The fire blazed, eating ravenously at the grass, eager to force the now running steers further and further towards the escarpment. Frightened steers moved faster; cowboys kept pace, choking on the dust from the flaying hooves and the burning smoke which threatened to suffocate.

Jim wondered about Seth. He would have expected him to take the lead and go to Eagle Point but the cattle had only just got moving when he saw Seth move alongside the steers, between them and the edge of the precipice! He was going to make the most dangerous ride of all! Pressure on the lead cattle from that side might help to turn them. Seth stabbed his horse faster. After only a moment's hesitation Jim followed. The cattle were moving faster and faster. At this speed would the men at Eagle Point stand a chance?

Once they reached Eagle Point the five men were out of their saddles and securing their horses amongst a small group of rocks at the point itself. They drew their rifles from their scabbards, and Lance quickly deployed them in the position he thought they stood the best chance of turning the herd. Smoke blew across their vision, and heat from the flames fanned in their direction, sending rivulets of sweat down their faces. Anxious and tense each man gripped his rifle and waited. Time seemed never ending. Dryness gripped their throats. Parched tongues tried to bring relief to dry lips.

Suddenly two riders burst from the smoke and turned into the gap. Lance saw them put their slickers into use as they moved across the edge of the fire.

Then a thunderous sound grew louder and louder, pounding nearer and nearer, rising above the crackle of the devouring flames. It beat frighteningly into the mind. Lance glanced at the men on each side of him. He saw the nervousness and fear. He didn't blame them for their feelings and he wouldn't have condemned them if they had chosen to run, to get their horses and escape the thunderous hell which was sweeping towards them. He wouldn't have branded them for he too felt a coward at this moment. He felt the sweat of his palms on the rifle and found himself slowly wiping each in turn down his shirt. That action seemed to bring a calmness to him. He gripped his rifle and waited.

As Seth moved steadily past the cattle there were times when he was perilously close to the edge of the escarpment. Choking dust rose around him almost clouding his view, but he rode desperately on; the cattle must be turned. He twisted, checked and urged to avoid the catastrophe which threatened him. All the time he drove relentlessly onwards, sending his horse faster and faster to outpace the herd. The dust cleared and Seth found himself alongside the lead steers. Steadily he put pressure to bear on the nearest animal but as they thundered on he seemed to be having little effect.

Suddenly he was aware of another rider close to him, helping, skilfully handling his horse, pressuring the steers. Seth was surprised to see Jim, but there was no time for acknowledgement, the grimness of the task required their full attention.

The extra help brought some measure

of result. The gap between the tearing hooves and the escarpment widened. But it needed more; Eagle Point was coming up fast.

Suddenly Seth's horse swerved, stumbled and lost its footing, sending its rider flying over its neck. Seth hit the ground hard and rolled towards the edge of the escarpment. Horror gripped Jim when he saw his father's horse falter. He hauled hard on his reins, bringing his horse round towards Seth. As the animal slithered, Jim flung himself from the saddle towards his father. He grabbed him and, as he helped him upright, he saw death-flaying hooves thunder down on them. There was only one hope. In desperation, Jim flung himself over the escarpment, dragging Seth with him.

They were falling, falling, still locked together. Jim's mind whirled. They had been unlucky, the drop was going to be too great. Then suddenly the breath was driven from his body as he thumped into the ground. He felt himself rolling. The landing had been softer than he had expected. Luck had held. A shale fall spreading out ten feet below the escarpment had taken their fall. As the two men rolled, stones and earth tumbled with them. Desperately they clawed to stop their slide. They slowed, and Jim twisted himself so that he was sliding feet first. A glance downward told him that they were still in trouble, the slope of shale ended abruptly in another drop!

Jim dug his feet in to slow up his slide. Seth bumped against him and Jim grabbed the big man, yelling to him to dig his feet in. Seth automatically did as he was told, and, while Jim held him, Seth used his hands to try to slow them down. The flesh was lacerated and torn from his fingers, but he felt no pain in the desperate clawing for survival. Suddenly his hands found a grip which jerked them to a stop with a suddenness which sent pain screaming through Seth's arms. But he hung on. Quickly Jim eased his weight off his father and found his own support and both men lay gasping for breath.

A few moments later they were able to take stock of the situation and found that they were about three quarters of the way down the shale slope. To try to make their way upwards would bring the danger of slipping back and the possibility of a death plunge at the bottom of the slope.

Seth glanced at Jim. "Thanks," he gasped. "Better stay put. The men at Eagle Point probably saw what happened."

The mention of Eagle Point brought the fate of the herd sharply to them. They listened intently, staring at each other as they did so.

The sound of pounding hooves still came to them; it was quieter but it was still there!

A grin broke across Seth's face. "They're still runnin' Jim! They've turned them!"

Jim found himself grinning in reply, he found himself pleased and he wondered why.

Lance bit at his bottom lip. This must go right, whatever happened they must not fail. Suddenly he started. A horseman appeared alongside the steers. His father! He was trying to turn them, to help his men when they had opened fire. Then things happened so fast that Lance hardly had time to grasp what they were. Another rider appeared, Jim! His father fell and then Jim was there out of the saddle and flinging them both out of the way of the thundering herd and over the cliff. Lance had no more time to think; the steers were pounding on.

He raised his rifle and took careful aim at the lead steer nearest the escarpment. He squeezed the trigger, and, immediately heard rifle fire break out on either side of him. The steer faltered, pitched to the ground and rolled over. Lance was already firing at the next one, and it too hit the ground. The steers immediately behind could not avoid the dead cattle and plunged into them with a bellowing cry of fear. Steers swerved to avoid the tumbled mass pressing hard on those next to them. The pressure was felt along the whole line as steers gave way. This coupled with the rapid rifle fire ahead started to swing the herd. Lance yelled to his men to keep it up. He leaped to his feet and the other four men joined him, adding another frightening obstacle to the cattle. They began to swerve even more, and then the leaders were round, plunging for the gap between the fire and the escarpment, and the whole herd followed. The earth shook, dust rose, clods were torn beneath flaying hooves but the herd was saved. Lance stopped his firing. He breathed more freely. They had done it! The cattle could be left to run themselves out across the prairie, but at least they would be safe. Some would be lost, trampled to death if they fell, or flung over the cliff if they lost their footing on the edge, but complete annihilation had been averted.

As soon as the last steer had passed,

the Running W men were racing to the spot where they had seen their boss and horse wrangler plunge over the edge.

They were panting heavily when they reached the place but were relieved to see two figures clinging to the slope.

"Hang on. We'll soon hev you up," yelled Lance. He turned to two of the men, "The horses, quick."

The men raced off and were soon back with the horses. Lance removed his lariat and swirling it above his head, sent it over the slope. It dropped just in front of the two men. Jim eased himself upwards. A foot slipped, sending stones showering downwards. He reached out, strained more and then his fingers closed round the rope. He pulled it the necessary few feet and slipped it round Seth's shoulders and under his arms. He waved his arm, indicating they were ready.

On seeing the signal, Lance turned the rope round his saddle-horn and told one of the men to mount. "Gently does it," he said. The man eased his horse forward foot by foot, and Seth, helping all he could, was pulled slowly up the slope.

Another rope had already been thrown by Dick Woods to Jim and a similar procedure was adopted to get him up. By the time they reached the last precipitous ten feet of rock, both men were on their feet and able to fend themselves off the jagged, cutting rocks, as the horses pulled them upwards. Eager hands reached to help them over the edge.

Seth and Jim lay gasping for breath as the ropes were slipped from them.

"You all right, pa?" asked Lance anxiously, as he gripped Seth's shoulder firmly with affection.

"Sure," grinned Seth, "except fer cuts an' bruises an' these." He held out his lacerated, flesh-torn hands.

Lance winced. "We'll git you home and git the doc." He helped his father to his feet. "How about you, Jim?"

"I'm not so bad," replied Jim.

"You'd better come back with us an'

189

hev the doc look at you," said Seth. "An' thanks fer savin' my life, it might hev cost you yours."

Jim met Seth's gaze but did not reply. He turned to the men with the horses, "Thanks fer gettin' mine."

"He ran out to Eagle Point," explained the cowboy. "I picked him up with the others."

"Let's git out of here," called Lance. "This fire won't stop until it reaches this edge." He sent one of the men to tell the doctor to come to the Running W, then helped his father into the saddle, swung up behind him, and they headed for the ranch.

"Mighty brave thing thet Jim did," commenced Lance.

"Sure was," agreed Seth. "Can't figure it out. Things point to him workin' with the Lazy A. Almost confirmed by you after following him last night."

"We'll know that after we move the horses. If they're attacked then we know Jim managed to get a message to — " He stopped, horrified by the thought which had just struck him. He pulled his horse to a halt. "The horses, pa! There's no one with them!"

"Dick!" yelled Seth. The cowboy swung his horse and rode over to the boss. "Get back to the horses as quickly as possible," he instructed. "It may be too late — the Lazy A may hev got them."

Dick Woods did not wait any longer. The urgency was not lost on him. Earth flew as he put his horse into a gallop.

"But they can't hev known about the fire to take advantage of it," said Lance.

"Can't they?" replied Seth. "They started it!"

"What!" Lance was completely surprised by the information. It was something he hadn't even thought of.

"By sheer chance, I sent a couple of the men out early this morning. They saw three Lazy A men firing the prairie. They were goin' after them but came back here to warn us. How did you spot it?"

"You've started me thinking," mused Lance. "It was Jim who saw it, an' now I come to think of it, he pushed the point of tryin' to git a few more better horses and rode to the top to see if he could spot the herd."

"An' he saw the fire instead and drew your attention to it," said Seth.

"Yes," confirmed Lance. "Deliberate to git us away from the horses."

"Could be," replied Seth. "We'll know when Dick gits back, an' then it might be time for some straight answers from Jim Benson."

"So Howley probably hoped to finish us off in one swoop, cattle destroyed and the horses scattered again so we couldn't fulfil the army contract."

When Jim saw Dick Woods answer Seth's call and then leave he figured that there was concern about the horses. When Seth got his answer there would be trouble and, with suspicion already directed against him, Jim figured the Running W would be no place for him.

His thoughts were confused as he recalled his action when he saw his father in danger. Why had he saved him when he could have seen revenge fulfilled? His mind raced, but suddenly he realized that he had never heard his mother condemn his father; never call for retribution. Maybe she didn't want revenge, maybe if she had been alive she wouldn't have condemned him for what he had done. Jim began to regret his actions. He would get out as soon as the opportunity arose, try and forget what he had done to a family he liked, and hope he had made up something by saving Seth's life. He would ride into town, leave a message with Sally for Jed to inform the Howleys that he was through — finished.

They were nearing the ranch-house when Lance put a suggestion to his father.

"Dick's answer won't give us complete proof against Jim, but, if I could confirm that Jim got a message to Howleys yesterday and thet he's done it before, then we've got him. As soon as you're in the house I'll ride into town."

His father approved. "You may hev to pay fer information, git some money out of the safe." As they neared the buildings he called out. "Jim, I'll send the doctor over to the bunk-house." Jim acknowledged with a wave of his hand. "Now you can git away without him knowin'," Seth said over his shoulder to Lance.

As soon as he could Lance left the Running W for Mineral Wells, hoping to find the truth from Sally.

Ten minutes later Jim was uneasy. The doctor hadn't arrived and, if Dick Woods returned with the news that the horses were missing, he may not get a chance to get away. Judging the men in the bunk-house to be preoccupied, Jim slipped unnoticed outside, got his horse and, after riding quietly from the buildings, put it into a fast gallop towards Mineral Wells.

9

WHEN Lance reached the saloon he wasted no time, so when his enquiry for Sally from the barman brought the answer that she was in her room, he went straight there.

"Well, this is a surprise; Lance Blackwell paying a call on me." Sally flashed a broad, inviting smile as she came close to Lance and gently shut the door behind him. "What's it to be Lance? Or is this sort of room new to you?" Lance looked embarrassed. Sally laughed. "Come on, sit down and have a drink first."

"Look, Sally, all I want is information," said Lance.

"Information? What about?"

"Jim Benson."

"Jim Benson? Your horse wrangler? Now what can I tell you about him?"

"Has he been seein' you since he

started workin' for the Running W?"

"What if he has? Has it anything to do with you what your men do in their spare time?"

"It might have, Sally, if it causes any trouble."

"Trouble?"

"Did he see you yesterday?"

"Now look here, Lance, Jim's a nice fella. I wouldn't — "

"Sally, it's important. I'll pay well for information." He saw a flash of interest in Sally's eyes. "Five hundred dollars!"

Sally sat down on the bed. "Five hundred dollars!" The words came in a whisper of amazement. "I like Jim, but — " She looked up at Lance. "You know I could hev fallen for him, told him so. Had a hope he might take me out of here one day, but he wasn't really interested to go that far, so — who turns down five hundred dollars?" She paused, pursed her lips thoughtfully then added, "Provided he doesn't get to know."

"He won't," answered Lance. "Now, was Jim here yesterday?"

"Yes."

"I followed him into town but lost him."

"I know, he sent me out to check who followed him."

Lance nodded. "So you came back in here and told him."

"Not in here. He was out back with Jed Simmons."

Lance smiled. Now he knew how he had missed seeing Jim. "What did he want with him?"

"Don't know."

"Has he contacted Jed before?"

"Yes," Sally went on to tell Lance what had happened previously and the evidence against Jim began to pile up.

"You don't know what was discussed between them?" asked Lance.

"Not the details," replied Sally, "but I have an idea."

"What's that?" asked Lance, eagerly.

Sally looked shrewdly at Lance. "This is from another source. Reckon it don't come under that five hundred."

Lance smiled. "All right, another hundred."

Sally smiled back. "I like a man who knows when he's onto a good thing and knows how to pay for it. Jed asked me to check on Jim, try to find out about his past. Told me it could help in what was happening between Jim and the Lazy A to get at the Running W."

Now Lance had all he wanted to know but he put one more question. "Did you find out anything about him?"

"Not yet. Haven't had the opportunity."

Lance fished six hundred dollars from his pocket and was handing it over to Sally when the door was flung open.

Jed kept his horse to a steady pace towards Mineral Wells. Things had gone well for the Howleys. Jim had taken the men away from the horses and that left the way open for the Lazy A men to scatter them. Seth Blackwell couldn't fulfil his contract now. If the fire had succeeded in destroying the cattle, one way or another, Seth Blackwell would be facing ruin. Jed would soon know; Jim would probably be on his way to Mineral Wells now.

Jed slipped from the saddle outside the saloon, tied his horse to the rail and went inside. He crossed to the bar.

"Jim Benson will be comin' in here sometime soon I guess, tell him I'm up in Sally's room." He started from the bar.

"Hold it Jed. There's someone up there already," said the barman.

"Who?" asked Jed sharply.

"Lance Blackwell."

Jed hid his surprise. He moved towards the stairs. Here was his chance to get Lance Blackwell. Chuck Howley would pay him well. As he reached the door of Sally's room he drew his Colt. Without pausing he flung open the door and stepped inside.

Lance and Sally turned, startled at the sudden intrusion.

"Blackwell!" The word snarled from Jed's throat.

There was no mistaking his intention. Sally seized with alarm jumped forward. "Jed, it's not what you — "

The crash of the Colt reverberated round the room. The words were cut short on Sally's lips and a look of disbelief and horror crossed her face. She staggered forward, reaching out for support on Jed. Lance's sudden immobility unfroze. He seized the slight opportunity offered to him. In one leap he was through the window, sending glass shattering in all directions. He hit the sloping roof of the lean-to adjoining the saloon. Wood split but it broke Lance's fall. He fell through on to a heap of sacks. It took only a moment for him to gather his wits, then he was on his feet tearing open the door. He ran along the alley pausing at the end to check the main street.

People were flocking towards the saloon after hearing the shot, but there was no sign of Jed.

A shot crashed in the saloon. Lance froze momentarily. What was happening?

It was no concern of his. He had the information he wanted. He must get out of Mineral Wells before Jed came looking for him.

He walked quickly to his horse, watching the saloon batwings for the appearance of Jed. Lance moved through people heading for the saloon. He reached his horse, unhitched it from the rail, led it a few yards along the street and, with one more precautionary glance around, mounted and rode out of town.

Jim kept a fast pace to Mineral Wells. He wanted to put as much ground between himself and the Running W as possible before Dick's return. After contacting Jed, and pulling out of the deal, he would get as far from Mineral Wells as he could.

He slowed as he entered town but kept to a brisk pace along the main street. There was no room at the rail outside the saloon so Jim tied his horse on the opposite side of the dust road. He crossed the street and, as he was mounting the steps in front of the batwings, a shot rang out from the saloon. Jim's step faltered only momentarily, then he was beside the doorpost peering over the batwings. By a swift glance he saw everyone in the saloon staring up at the balcony. Jim stepped inside quickly. He stopped, horrified, at the sight of Jed, with gun in hand, stepping backwards out of Sally's room. Sally was trying to desperately to cling to Jed who was attempting to shake her off. As he stepped on to the balcony he freed himself of Sally's grip and she slumped face downwards on to the floor.

Sally, murdered by Jed! Jim's thoughts whirled. Anger rose inside him. He clawed at his gun. Jed started to run for the stairs. Jim moved swiftly between the tables and reached the bottom of the stairs as Jed turned to come down.

"Hold it!" rapped Jim.

Jed suddenly realized what it must look like. "I didn't — " He kept on coming, and Jim's Colt drove lead into Jed's shoulder. A second shot took him in the stomach. He twisted and spun backwards to fall on the balcony. His Colt spun from his grasp. Jim took the stairs two at a time.

"You scum," snarled Jim, as he stood over Jed.

"Fool!" gasped Jed, glaring angrily at Jim. "I was tryin' for Lance Blackwell, Sally got in the way!" He winced with pain.

"What!" Jim's brain pounded. Lance here! Why?

"If — if — " Jed coughed. Pain racked his body. His voice went to a whisper. Jim dropped to his knees. "You don't — deserve it," spluttered Jed weakly. "But if you — get — Lance — you'll be in — good with Chuck." He gasped, flopped back on the floor and lay still.

Jim stared at the body. Jed's words beat in his mind. Then suddenly he was aware of the noise in the saloon and of people running up the stairs.

He rose from his knees as the sheriff, Colt in hand, reached him.

"What happened?" asked the lawman.

"Jed shot Sally," said Jim.

Both men moved quickly to the girl. One glance told them she was dead.

"Heard Lance Blackwell's name mentioned as I ran through the saloon," commented the sheriff. He stepped into Sally's room. From the doorway Jim saw the broken window. "He went through thet window," said the sheriff. He came back on to the balcony and called to one of his deputies. "Git round to the lean-to, see if anyone's there." The man pushed his way through the crowd at the foot of the stairs. "Right, Jim, tell me what you know."

Jim related what he knew of the shooting but omitted Jed's reason for wanting to kill Lance. Jim was anxious. He wanted to be away. Lance was in danger, possibly from any Lazy A cowboy seeking his boss's favour. Lance must be warned. Jim watched anxiously for the return of the deputy as he told his story.

"Seems like a case of jealousy," commented the sheriff. "Sorry you killed him, Jim, but it was understandable under the circumstances."

Jim nodded and turned to see the deputy mounting the stairs.

"No one there," he reported.

"When you git back to the Running W tell Lance to stay there. I'll be out to see him after I'm through here. It will only be a formality."

Jim nodded and hurried down the stairs. He crossed the street, unhitched his horse and climbed into the saddle. He hesitated before turning the animal. He could ride away and try to forget he had ever come to Mineral Wells, had ever found his father. But could he? Wouldn't memories haunt him for the rest of his life? Wouldn't he wonder and, maybe regret that he hadn't warned Lance of Chuck Howley's intention? But if he rode back to the Running W he'd be riding into a heap of trouble himself.

While Kathy helped her mother bathe her father's wounds, her thoughts were occupied with their troubles. She kept coming back to the same conclusion that none of this would have happened if she had agreed to marry Chuck Howley.

Suddenly Kathy started for the door. "I'm going to see Chuck," she called.

Astonished, Seth and Martha exchanged glances.

"Kathy!" Seth's voice boomed. She stopped with her hand on the door and turned. "You'll do no such thing."

"You were nearly killed today," said Kathy. "I'm going to put a stop to all this." She did not wait to hear any more but swung out of the door and hurried out of the house.

"Stop her, Martha," said Seth.

Martha did not move but looked lovingly into her husband's eyes. "It won't do any good," she said quietly.

"She'll be all right. Let her go. She'll see things differently when she get's back."

The doctor came, attended to Seth and then went to the bunk-house to see Jim. A few minutes later the doctor was confronting Seth with the news that Jim was not there.

"One of your men checked the stable for me, thought he might be there. He wasn't and his horse has gone," concluded the doctor.

"All right, doc," said Seth. "If he needs lookin' at, I'll send him into town."

The doctor left Seth wondering why a stranger should come to him and then sell him out to Howley.

The pound of a hard ridden horse took Seth and Martha on to the verandah. Lance, now they would soon know.

Lance was out of the saddle almost before the horse had stopped.

"Jim was passin' information to the Lazy A." He panted his news as he strode on to the verandah.

"Did Sally say why?" asked Seth.

"Didn't know," replied Lance. He went on to tell his mother and father all the information which Sally had given him. As he was speaking it struck him suddenly that Kathy wasn't there. It was strange, for she would most certainly have wanted to hear his news. "Where's Kathy?" he asked.

"She went to the Lazy A," said his mother.

"What!" Lance was annoyed. "What for?"

"She figured on tryin' to put a stop to their attacks," explained Seth. "We tried to stop her but — "

"Then I will," cut in Lance. "She mustn't sacrifice herself." He swung down from the verandah and was into the saddle almost before Martha and Seth realized it. Ignoring his father's call he put his horse into a gallop in the direction of the Lazy A.

Seth stared after him for a moment then turned to his wife. "I'm goin' to stop them," he said. He turned but was pulled up short by the pain in his leg.

"Seth, you can't go," said Martha. "You're in no fit state to ride. You couldn't hold the reins with hands like yours." She took her husband's arm. "Come on." She turned him gently towards the door. "All we can do is wait, and that can be very hard, wondering what is happening."

"But, Martha, if anything should happen to either of them I — "

"Nothing will happen." Martha tried to sound reassuring.

They went back into the house and it was an impatient and uneasy Seth who listened intently for the sound of their return.

Time was passing too slowly for Seth who suddenly stiffened in his chair. "Martha, they're comin'."

Martha listened. She heard nothing and looked questioningly at her husband, who raised his hand indicating her not to make a sound.

"There!" he suddenly said, and Martha heard the faint sound of hooves. They hurried outside. The sound was nearer. Seth turned and looked questioningly at Martha. "There's one horse comin' from town," observed Seth. There was no disguising the disappointment in his voice.

They leaned on the rail waiting for the rider to come into sight. Then the horse was there, coming at a fast run straight towards the ranch-house. Seth's hands gripped the rail tightly until the whites of his knuckles showed. Martha could feel the tension in her husband. "Benson," he whispered in a low voice, but one which was full of hatred for the rider. "Martha get my gun."

"No! Seth, No!" cried Martha.

"This man sold us out, he deserves — "

"To be heard first," cut in Martha tersely.

Seth bit his lip hard. He turned to go for his gun but Martha restrained him. "He'll be here and gone by the time you get it," she said.

"You'd warn him?" roared Seth.

"I want no killing," replied Martha quietly but firmly. "I nearly lost you once today and remember Jim saved your life." Seth frowned but said nothing. He had to stay if he wanted to confront Jim Benson.

"What the hell do you want?" yelled Seth as Jim hauled his horse to a dust-stirring halt.

Jim knew instantly that Seth realized or guessed about his relations with the Howleys.

"Where's Lance?" Jim shouted back.

"Git down off thet horse," shouted Seth. "I want some answers to a few questions."

Jim steadied his horse. "Has Lance been back here from Mineral Wells?" he asked.

"He sure has an' he's got the information about you an' Howley — "

"Didn't he tell you Jed Simmons tried to kill him?"

"No!" Seth and Martha glanced at each other in alarm.

"On Chuck Howley's instructions, but Lance doesn't realize this," went on Jim. "Now, where is he, he must be told."

There was something about Jim's attitude, about the tone of his voice which impressed Seth that, in spite of what he knew about Jim, the horse wrangler was genuine in his concern for Lance.

"He's gone to Lazy A to try to stop Kathy giving in to Chuck!" said Seth.

"What!" Jim didn't wait to hear any more. He wheeled his horse and left in a cloud of dust for the Lazy A.

As much as Jim wanted to reach the Lazy A as quickly as possible he slowed his ride when the ranch was in sight so as not to draw undue attention to himself.

He rode openly, risking being stopped and hoping no one in the house would see his approach. No one bothered him, one man was of no significance.

Jim was out of the saddle quickly.

He stepped on to the verandah quietly and, opening the front door without knocking, went into the house. As he closed the door quietly he drew his Colt. He paused, listening intently. A low sound of voices came from the door on the right. Jim moved stealthily to it and listened.

"You won't git away with it, Howley." It was Lance's voice.

"I will but you won't be here to know," laughed Chuck. "It was a good job I was outside when you arrived, your sister doesn't even know you're here. So we can go quietly off, an' you can be dealt with, an' the way you'll be found will indicate an accident on the trail. All very nice an' convenient. You out of the way, I marry Kathy an' the Running W will be mine."

"You low-down — "

"Cut the heroics," snapped Chuck. "You've tried to stall this long enough, Kathy and pa will be wondering when I'm comin' back."

So those two were alone! Jim seized

on the fact and flung open the door. Chuck whirled, startled at the sudden intrusion. He gasped when he saw Jim with gun drawn.

"Jim, what the — ?" he started.

"You ain't doin' any killin', Chuck!" Jim's voice was cold.

"Keep out of this, Benson!" rapped Chuck.

The door of the room across the hall was flung open and Pete Howley ran out followed by Kathy. They both pulled up in surprise. Pete clawed at his gun but Kathy seeing his action, flung herself against him, sending him off balance. Jim's attention was diverted for a split second by the sudden appearance of Pete and Kathy. Chuck seized that instance and squeezed the trigger.

Almost at that moment, Jim realized his concentrated attention on Howley had wavered and he flung himself sideways. He felt a sharp pain through his side. He fired at the crouching form and saw it jerk. A look of disbelief crossed Chuck's face. He staggered backwards but a table stopped him. As Jim hit the floor, his hand caught a chair and jerked his Colt from his grip. Chuck's knees began to buckle. He raised his Colt at the defenceless Jim, but before he could aim, Lance crashed at him sending him to the floor. He tried to get up but Jim's bullet had death on it and Chuck collapsed into a silent heap. Two steps took Lance into the hall where Kathy was still struggling on the floor with Pete.

"Hold it!" rapped Lance.

The struggle stopped and Pete found himself facing the threatening muzzle of a Colt.

Kathy scrambled to her feet and, when Pete got up she removed his Colt.

"All right, Howley, this is the end," snapped Lance.

Pete shrugged his shoulders as he stared into the room at his dead son. "Seems like it," he said dejectedly. "What a tangle friends can git into over their children." A voice from outside the front caught his attention.

He glanced at Lance. "I could do fer you yet," he said, "but what's the use now?" He moved to the front door, and opened it. Lance kept him covered. "All right," called out Pete to the Lazy A men who were rushing to the house. "Chuck's dead, but thet's the end. No molestin' the Blackwells when they ride out of here." He turned back into the house. "There you are," he said wearily. "Put your gun away." He walked slowly into the room and dropped on his knees beside his son.

As Kathy helped Jim into the hall she glanced at Lance. "Let's go," she said. "Jim needs attention. Think you can ride?" Jim nodded. He would have to go back to the Running W; he wished he could ride away.

Relief flooded over Martha and Seth when they saw Kathy and Lance riding towards the house. Lance helped Jim from his horse, refusing to answer questions until he had got the horse wrangler inside.

Martha examined the wound pronouncing it as a flesh wound which she would soon attend to but warned that Jim would answer no questions until she had fixed him up.

Lance and Kathy explained what had happened.

"I tried to get Chuck to call the whole thing off," explained Kathy, "but when he said the only way was to marry him I eventually agreed. He left me talking to his father and the next thing was the shooting. I was surprised to see Lance and Jim."

"I came to try to stop you Kathy but Chuck jumped me, took me into the opposite room to you. He was goin' to get me out of the way so that when he married you he would get the Running W. Then Jim arrived." He went on to explain about the shooting.

"We are in your debt again, Jim," said Seth. "That's twice today you've saved the life of a member of this family."

"How did you know Chuck wanted

rid of me?" asked Lance.

Jim explained about his visit to Mineral Wells and of his encounter with Jed. "I expect you were there to find out about me," he concluded.

"Yes," replied Lance.

"Then you know I was workin' with the Howleys?"

"Yes, but why?" asked Seth. "It doesn't add up. You help the Howleys to try to destroy us yet you save our lives at the risk of your own."

Jim hesitated. He glanced round the four people awaiting his answer. "I guess it does seem confused, an' I guess I was mixed up too. At times I didn't know whether I wanted to go on with the Howleys or try to undo the things I had done. After the fire I decided to leave, partly because I knew you were checking on me. I was going on from Mineral Wells after I'd told Jed I was pullin' out of the deal. Well, you know what happened there an' I couldn't let Lance go in ignorance of his danger." He paused.

"You still haven't told us why," said Kathy.

"For over a year I sought a man for revenge. I found him. Then I found I liked his family and there were things in him I admired. I finally decided I couldn't work against him any longer when I saw his courage and bravery in taking the most dangerous job, when trying to turn his cattle frightened by the fire."

The four people stared at him incredulously.

"Me!" gasped Seth. Jim nodded. "But why? I don't know you. What wrong have I ever done you?"

Jim met Seth's gaze firmly. "You deprived me of a father and you killed my mother!"

"What! I've never killed anyone in my life, man or woman," replied Seth.

"I didn't say you killed my father. As for my mother, you never raised a hand against her but you surely killed her."

Seth's annoyance was beginning to rise and Martha sensed it. "Jim," she said. "Give it to us straight."

Jim looked hard at Seth. "Remember Elkhorn?"

Seth gasped. This was a name he had never expected to hear again. "Yes, I used to live there."

"You walked out on your wife and son!"

Seth was astounded and it showed on his face. "I left Elkhorn, yes, but I didn't walk out on them, I intended to send for them when I got settled, but they died in a fever epidemic."

It was Jim's turn to be surprised. He stared incredulously at his father. He remembered the fever epidemic, his mother had been ill but —

"Word reached me that the whole town had been wiped out. There was no point in going back." Seth's words broke into Jim's thoughts.

"There would have been. Your wife and son were alive!"

Seth stared at Jim disbelievingly. "But — I — How do you know?" Something of the truth was beginning to dawn on Seth. "Jim. My son was called Jim. You — " Seth faltered. "Are you Jim Blackwell?"

Jim met his father's gaze and nodded. There was silence. The moments were charged with incredulity, disbelief and the realization of the enormity of this acknowledgement.

Seth looked at Martha, Kathy, Lance and then back to Martha searching for some assurance. "What, what can I say?" he asked.

Martha moved closer to him and took his hand. Seth felt a warmth, a feeling that this made no difference to Martha, she loved him and there was no altering that.

Jim felt in his pocket and took out a locket. "This may prove it."

Seth took the locket from him and his mind tumbled back over the years to the last time he had seen it round the throat of Mary when he kissed her goodbye.

He looked at Jim. "What have I done? Your mother when — ?"

"She died just over a year ago, brought early by a hard life."

"And you thought I'd walked out on you!" gasped Seth. "Can you ever forgive me? Would she ever forgive me?"

"Now I know the reason why you didn't return, I can," replied Jim. "As for Ma, she never said one word against you, the bitterness was all in me for what it had done to her."

"Thank God for that small comfort," said Seth quietly.

Martha smiled at Jim. "Now, you'll stay. This must be home, son."

"Thanks," replied Jim. "But how can I after what I've done. Pa, can you ever forgive me?"

"You saved my life, and Lance's twice — that's more than repayment. Our losses can be made up, our lives would have been gone forever but for you. You must stay, you must be one of us." He looked for approval from Kathy and Lance who were not slow in impressing Jim that he was wanted.

Seth held out his hand. "Welcome home son."

Jim smiled. The word he had always longed to hear had been said.

"You're all so kind," he said. "There's only one regret in all this." He looked at Kathy. "Now, you know why I was afraid of our feelings becoming too close, sister."

Kathy smiled. "But I'm not your sister. You see your father is not my father. Mother was a widow with two children when your father met her."

THE END

Other titles in the
Linford Western Library:

TOP HAND
Wade Everett

The Broken T was big. But no ranch is big enough to let a man hide from himself.

GUN WOLVES OF LOBO BASIN
Lee Floren

The Feud was a blood debt. When Smoke Talbot found the outlaws who gunned down his folks he aimed to nail their hide to the barn door.

SHOTGUN SHARKEY
Marshall Grover

The westbound coach carrying the indomitable Larry and Stretch headed for a shooting showdown.

FIGHTING RAMROD
Charles N. Heckelmann

Most men would have cut their losses, but Frazer counted the bullets in his guns and said he'd soak the range in blood before he'd give up another inch of what was his.

LONE GUN
Eric Allen

Smoke Blackbird had been away too long. The Lequires had seized the Blackbird farm, forcing the Indians and settlers off, and no one seemed willing to fight! He had to fight alone.

THE THIRD RIDER
Barry Cord

Mel Rawlins wasn't going to let anything stand in his way. His father was murdered, his two brothers gone. Now Mel rode for vengeance.

ARIZONA DRIFTERS
W. C. Tuttle

When drifting Dutton and Lonnie Steelman decide to become partners they find that they have a common enemy in the formidable Thurston brothers.

TOMBSTONE
Matt Braun

Wells Fargo paid Luke Starbuck to outgun the silver-thieving stagecoach gang at Tombstone. Before long Luke can see the only thing bearing fruit in this eldorado will be the gallows tree.

HIGH BORDER RIDERS
Lee Floren

Buckshot McKee and Tortilla Joe cut the trail of a border tough who was running Mexican beef into Texas. They stopped the smuggler in his tracks.

BRETT RANDALL, GAMBLER
E. B. Mann

Larry Day had the choice of running away from the law or of assuming a dead man's place. No matter what he decided he was bound to end up dead.

THE GUNSHARP
William R. Cox

The Eggerleys weren't very smart. They trained their sights on Will Carney and Arizona's biggest blood bath began.

THE DEPUTY OF SAN RIANO
Lawrence A. Keating and
Al. P. Nelson

When a man fell dead from his horse, Ed Grant was spotted riding away from the scene. The deputy sheriff rode out after him and came up against everything from gunfire to dynamite.

FARGO: MASSACRE RIVER
John Benteen

The ambushers up ahead had now blocked the road. Fargo's convoy was a jumble, a perfect target for the insurgents' weapons!

SUNDANCE: DEATH IN THE LAVA
John Benteen

The Modoc's captured the wagon train and its cargo of gold. But now the halfbreed they called Sundance was going after it . . .

HARSH RECKONING
Phil Ketchum

Five years of keeping himself alive in a brutal prison had made Brand tough and careless about who he gunned down . . .

FARGO: PANAMA GOLD
John Benteen

With foreign money behind him, Buckner was going to destroy the Panama Canal before it could be completed. Fargo's job was to stop Buckner.

FARGO: THE SHARPSHOOTERS
John Benteen

The Canfield clan, thirty strong were raising hell in Texas. Fargo was tough enough to hold his own against the whole clan.

PISTOL LAW
Paul Evan Lehman

Lance Jones came back to Mustang for just one thing — revenge! Revenge on the people who had him thrown in jail.

HELL RIDERS
Steve Mensing

Wade Walker's kid brother, Duane, was locked up in the Silver City jail facing a rope at dawn. Wade was a ruthless outlaw, but he was smart, and he had vowed to have his brother out of jail before morning!

DESERT OF THE DAMNED
Nelson Nye

The law was after him for the murder of a marshal — a murder he didn't commit. Breen was after him for revenge — and Breen wouldn't stop at anything . . . blackmail, a frameup . . . or murder.

DAY OF THE COMANCHEROS
Steven C. Lawrence

Their very name struck terror into men's hearts — the Comancheros, a savage army of cutthroats who swept across Texas, leaving behind a blood-stained trail of robbery and murder.

SUNDANCE: SILENT ENEMY
John Benteen

A lone crazed Cheyenne was on a personal war path. They needed to pit one man against one crazed Indian. That man was Sundance.

LASSITER
Jack Slade

Lassiter wasn't the kind of man to listen to reason. Cross him once and he'll hold a grudge for years to come — if he let you live that long.

LAST STAGE TO GOMORRAH
Barry Cord

Jeff Carter, tough ex-riverboat gambler, now had himself a horse ranch that kept him free from gunfights and card games. Until Sturvesant of Wells Fargo showed up.

McALLISTER ON THE COMANCHE CROSSING
Matt Chisholm

The Comanche, McAllister owes them a life — and the trail is soaked with the blood of the men who had tried to outrun them before.

QUICK-TRIGGER COUNTRY
Clem Colt

Turkey Red hooked up with Curly Bill Graham's outlaw crew. But wholesale murder was out of Turk's line, so when range war flared he bucked the whole border gang alone . . .

CAMPAIGNING
Jim Miller

Ambushed on the Santa Fe trail, Sean Callahan is saved by two Indian strangers. But there'll be more lead and arrows flying before the band join Kit Carson against the Comanches.

GUNSLINGER'S RANGE
Jackson Cole

Three escaped convicts are out for revenge. They won't rest until they put a bullet through the head of the dirty snake who locked them behind bars.

RUSTLER'S TRAIL
Lee Floren

Jim Carlin knew he would have to stand up and fight because he had staked his claim right in the middle of Big Ike Outland's best grass.

THE TRUTH ABOUT SNAKE RIDGE
Marshall Grover

The troubleshooters came to San Cristobal to help the needy. For Larry and Stretch the turmoil began with a brawl and then an ambush.

WOLF DOG RANGE
Lee Floren

Will Ardery would stop at nothing, unless something stopped him first — like a bullet from Pete Manly's gun.

DEVIL'S DINERO
Marshall Grover

Plagued by remorse, a rich old reprobate hired the Texas Troubleshooters to deliver a fortune in greenbacks to each of his victims.

GUNS OF FURY
Ernest Haycox

Dane Starr, alias Dan Smith, wanted to close the door on his past and hang up his guns, but people wouldn't let him.